AFRICA

ANNALISA CONTI

Published by AEC Publishing LLC in New York

www.annalisaconti.com

ISBN-13: 978-0-9965174-1-6
ISBN-10: 0996517413

AFRICA

To Emmanuel

CONTENTS

1   The End   1

2   Ashes To Ashes   7

3   Dark Tunnel   19

4   The Way Out   27

5   A Desert Of Dreams   39

6   Dead River   49

7   Dawn   59

8   Rise   65

9   Like A Flower In The Desert   77

10 The King Is Naked   85

11 War   93

12 Reality   101

13 Mirrors   107

14 My Country, My Place   115

15 Open Drawers   125

16 The Truth, Part One   133

17 The Truth, Part Two   145

18	Prepare To Live	157
19	Water	165
20	The Way Back	171
21	A New Beginning	177
	Acknowledgments	183
	About The Author	187

1 THE END

What's that noise? Is that the phone?

She opened her eyes and she sat up in her bed. Not much light coming in from behind the window shutters, it was still night outside. She kept listening, holding her breath: nothing. The phone was not ringing, after all.

She grabbed her mobile phone from the nightstand and she turned it on, asking herself what time it was; she had her answer after a few seconds: 3:27 am. She sighed and rubbed her forehead with a hand, then she decided to get some water from the kitchen; some lights were turned on, a glass was filled from the pitcher, and she sat on a bar stool at the kitchen countertop.

She held her face in her hands: How many times does this have to happen?, she asked herself, How many times do I have to wake up like this in the middle of the night? How many times does the phone have to ring in my head, again and again? She looked at the landline phone itself, tiny white thing, and suddenly she slid down the bar stool to unplug the phone from the wall, with all the resentment that she had accumulated against it in the previous two weeks. She sat down again on the bar stool, scrolling through Facebook on her mobile phone with her right thumb: pictures of people, smiling, crying, eating, travelling, whatever. She didn't care. She put her iPhone down again, and she went to the window to look outside: surprise, even New York City was empty sometimes. Another sigh. She picked up her mobile phone again and she tapped on the Facebook logo, to open the application and look for something she could care about. Nothing.

Not that she had never cared: there had been a time when she had cared about things - her family, her friends, her job, herself. She used to love all those things, just like normal people do, most of the time. She just didn't care *anymore*. She snorted and almost smiled about it: sometimes one detail can change everything, in just one second, and there's no turning back. There can't be any turning back; things don't just go back to where they were before other things happened: the two sets of *things* are just incompatible. There's no solution.

Everything was still very clear in her mind.

On that Thursday night, two weeks before, she had had dinner with Rachel, in a small West Village Spanish tapas bar. Rachel had always been her best friend: after going through college and more than ten years of working life, her closest friend was still the girl she had shared her room with in her first year at Columbia. They had always been very different, but that had never stopped them from being incredibly close. Rachel had always known what she wanted to do with her life, so she had gone to law school right after undergrad, and she was now a partner in a law firm. The two women hadn't seen each other for a couple of weeks, both too busy with work and life; even if they had exchanged emails and texts almost every day, Rachel had had a long series of office gossips to report that night: everyone seemed to sleep with everyone else in that office. Everyone but Rachel: That's the only line I draw, she always said, No colleagues. She had never had a serious long-term relationship, though, always finding herself stuck in wrong love affairs: that was the only thing in her life that Rachel hadn't been able to find a solution for, yet.

Rachel had whispered a particularly juicy story about a brand new junior associate who seemed too open minded even for that firm. During her first week in the job she had slept with one of her fellow junior colleagues, a British guy who had just moved to the US and already loved American girls. In her third week, the girl had spent several nights in the office with a female senior partner, working on a complicated case, and rumor had it she had done way more than unveiling the inner secrets of their client... but information had gotten more confused at that point. Rachel had laughed very hard that night at dinner, and the two friends had had a few more glasses of sangria in her colleague's honor. The girl clearly deserved them.

She had been quite tipsy when she had left the restaurant with Rachel, and she had decided to clean her head walking with her friend for a few minutes: Rachel's apartment was only a few blocks down from the restaurant. She had hugged Rachel in front of her door, and she had gone to the West 4 subway stop to catch a train that would have brought her back uptown. She hated West 4: the A C and the B D lines run on two different levels, and the voice that announces trains arriving on one level never says anything about trains on the other level. Anyone who lives in the Upper West Side, and wants to go home with whatever train comes first, has to wait in that sort of mezzanine limbo between the two levels, trying to look both up and down to see if anything shows up. Rats run up and down the stairs, too, but they never say much about what train they're trying to catch.

Once at home, she had barely had time to brush her teeth and throw her clothes on a chair, before passing out on her bed.

She had been dreaming drunken dreams when a noise had woken her up. What's that noise?

She hadn't been able to place it at first, and she had had to wait for it to happen again: ring!

- The phone! - She had said out loud.

For some reasons she hadn't turned the lights on, but she had instead decided to use the faint light coming from outside the windows to fumble to the kitchen, where the landline phone was screaming.

- Hello? - She had finally made it stop.

- Hello ma'am, am I talking to Miss Amber Stevens? - A female voice on the other side.

- Yes, that's me. Who's speaking?

- Hello Miss Stevens, this is Agent Fortuna from the NYPD, 105th Precinct in Queens, my ID number is 42160.

- Hello - Interesting introduction.

- Miss Stevens, I unfortunately have bad news for you.

As it sometimes happens, Amber had sobered up right that second.

- What's wrong agent? What happened?

- Miss Stevens, there has been a car accident, and we found your contact number on the Emergency ID Card of one of the victims.

She had held her breath until the woman on the other side had started to speak again.

- Miss Stevens, I want to make sure that you sit down right now, and try to keep calm.

Bad cop joke.

- Who died? - She had just asked.

- His name was Michael Gillingham, ma'am, I'm very sorry for...

- No no no - Amber had hysterically laughed - No no no Agent, Mike is here! I don't remember if I heard him opening the door and getting into bed, but I know he got back very late from the airport, and he's here now. He called me yesterday afternoon to tell me that his flight got delayed, and that I should go to sleep, because he would get back very late. But now he's here. I know he's here.

- Miss Stevens, calm down now. Mr. Gillingham had his wallet in his pocket, we are sure that's him.

- No no no - She had violently shaken her head - I'm telling you, he's here. Mike! - She had screamed, so that he could have heard her from the bedroom - Mike!

He hadn't answered, so she had just dropped the phone and rushed back to the bedroom. She had turned the lights on. The bed was empty.

She had run to the other bedroom, to see if he was still working at the desk or maybe he had fallen asleep on the couch. He was not there.

She had run back to their bedroom, grabbed her mobile phone and called him. In the meantime, she had gotten back to the kitchen and picked up again the landline receiver with her other hand:

- See, I'm calling him, Agent, he will pick up and everything will be clear.

- Miss Stevens, I have the victim's phone in my hand, and the incoming call says "Amber Stevens mobile".

- No no no, there must be a contact. Let me call him again.

She had hanged up and tapped on Mike's name again.

- See, he will answer now, it's ringing. Oh! He picked up!

- Miss Stevens - Agent Fortuna's voice had surrounded her, coming out with an overwhelming stereo effect from both the landline and her iPhone - I am very sorry for your loss.

2 ASHES TO ASHES

Two weeks are a really short time, if you compare them to a whole life. Yet, her last two weeks had somehow indefinitely expanded, and she felt like she had gotten ten years older all of a sudden. She was looking at her image in the mirror, that morning, after having woken up in the middle of the night and having then tried to get back to sleep for about four hours, just like every other night since Mike had died. There it was, the truth in front of her: Mike had died. Mike was dead. She couldn't even say it out loud yet, but she could see it in her own face: the corners of her mouth hopelessly facing down, accompanied by two long pale wrinkles, one on each cheek, that she was sure she had never had before. Her eyes were dry, empty: they were the eyes of a ghost, all their light was gone.

The mirror had shown her that same image every morning for the past two weeks: that face that she had never seen before, but that now she was starting to get familiar with; a person she could barely recognize, one who couldn't smile, who couldn't laugh, who couldn't even feel properly alive. Now every time she opened her eyes in the dark she hoped to be finally waking up from that horrible dream where Mike was gone and he had left her alone. But there is not waking up from reality, she told herself, This is reality. She wished she could remove that face from her sight, peal the skin off the bones and replace it with what she had been used to for so many years. Sometimes she wished she was dead.

She had already cried all her tears - what a very dramatic thing to say, it almost made her grin: she had read that in so many bad romance books, so many stupid blog posts. But it was true for her, that bad book contained her own story now: after she had received that call in the middle of the night, she hadn't been able to stop her tears from falling destructively from her eyes, leaving permanent scars on her face, for days and nights and then days again.

The policewoman had left the news of Mike's death floating in the air, and Amber had held the landline phone receiver in her hand for a few long seconds, barely breathing, staring at it as if it was an evil object. Teardrops had started to spill on it, and Amber hadn't been able to understand where they were coming from, at first: she was paralyzed with refusal. Her right hand had automatically started to tap on the numerical keys, while her left hand had been slowly approaching the receiver to her ear. When the female voice had picked up the phone on the other side, no words had come out of Amber's mouth, just a long lament.

- Amber? Amber, is that you? - Rachel's voice had sounded sleepy at first.

- Amber? Are you crying? Tell me what happened! - She had immediately guessed that something was wrong; she didn't know why, yet, but Rachel had felt like crying too.

Amber had been relieved to let herself collapse in Rachel's arms when her friend had reached her apartment in that darkest of nights. Her tears had kept flowing when her parents had gotten to her flat the following morning: she hadn't had the strength to stand that look on her mother's face, that mix of silent despair and anger for that rotten fate. She had screamed when the police had forced her to see his body, that day at the morgue, and she had tried to cover her eyes, a pathetic attempt to protect them, to protect herself. We need to identify him, they had said, We have to be sure. She had been sure, she would have recognized him even with her eyes closed, even with her eyes carved out of her face and thrown at the center of the Earth. For a moment she had thought about touching him, taking him in her arms for a last second, kissing his forehead for the last time, but then she had somehow shaken herself: He is gone, this is not Mike anymore, this is just a dead body. That hadn't helped.

She was dry now. She didn't have anything inside, anymore.

The eyes of the girl in the mirror were dull, her face was grey, her skin looked old, her... Her phone vibrated: a text from Rachel.

"I'm on my way, be there in five."

What?

"You coming here?", she replied.

"You forgot."

She checked her iPhone's calendar, and she found an invite for that morning at 9: apartment visit, 230 Bleecker Street, organizer Rachel.

"Can you reschedule?", she tried.

"No."

And a minute later: "I'm here.", and the intercom rang. Amber was still in the bathroom, and she took a final look at her face in the mirror: she looked horrible, she felt even worse.

- Hi dear - Rachel hugged her by the door and she let herself into the apartment - I knew I'd find you like this - She added, touching her pajama pants and making a disapproving sound with her mouth - So I came in a bit early.

- What time is it? - Amber asked.

- It's 7:30, almost sharp, and I brought you coffee and a gluten-free muffin.

- Oh please, not your gluten-free crap!

- It's good for you, Amber, eat. I can see you haven't eaten much in the past ten days.

The last time they had seen each other had been at Mike's funeral. Amber didn't remember much of it: a line of black shadows walking by her side, touching her shoulder with mumbling words of condolences, a procession of ghosts among which she had seen herself, too, a lost soul wishing to escape from a now useless body. She thought her brain was protecting her by deleting those memories, and she was thankful for it. She knew she had spent the following several days in bed: she hadn't eaten much, she hadn't showered much, she hadn't wanted to see anyone. Mike's parents had come to New York just for the funeral, and they had gone back to London shortly afterwards; Mike's mother had held Amber in a long hug, right before leaving, and she had whispered something in her ear. Amber couldn't remember what she had said: her sight had been blurry with tears, her ears must have forgotten. Mike's parents had always been so beautiful together: his mother was tall and elegant, her skin darker than the night and her eyes brighter than a sunny day; his father had the most charming smile that Amber had ever seen, and Irish freckles on his nose. I'll never see them again, she had thought.

- Amber? Are you awake?

- Yes, sorry - She replied, her thoughts lost somewhere in the past.

- Good, the bath is ready, and I brought you some of my clothes: I was not sure if you had anything clean here.

Rachel looked at her friend for another second, and then she added with a tender smile: - I think my clothes will be too big for you now, though, but we can give them a try after the bath.

- I don't need the bath, I'm fine…

- You do need it, trust me - Rachel looked at her with a very convincing expression on her face.

Amber went to the bathroom, she slowly got undressed and she put her feet in the bathtub, hot and sweet with foam.

- Do you want me to rub your back?

Amber almost smiled: - No thanks, but you can come here with me.

Rachel entered the restroom and she sat on the waste basket.

- You're going to break that: your ass got bigger.

- Oh look, what do we have here? Some actual humor? Oh my God! Some actual humor from a Vanity Fair journalist, who would have thought! - Rachel replied, bursting out in a very theatrical fake laugh, and almost falling from the waste basket. But she didn't break it, yet. Amber tried to smile back at her friend.

- It's good to see you smiling, or at least trying to - Rachel told her, scratching her friend's head - Now let's try to wash your hair.

Amber left her apartment for the first time in a very long period, so long that she didn't even remember what season it was outside: she thought it would already be summer, but it was still mid-April, not exactly warm. They reached the A B C D stop a few blocks away, and they jumped on a train.

- Where are we going?

- West 4 - Rachel replied.

- I hate West 4.

- I know, but once you'll live there you'll be just three blocks away from me, and you won't have to come all the way up here ever again!

- All the way up here? It's like fifteen minutes with the express!

- Yes, sure - Everything above 72nd street was already the Bronx for Rachel - Anyway, we are going to see three apartments in the same block, for sure we'll find something for you.

The village: she had always liked it for a Friday night, not so much for renting an apartment; but Rachel had spent her last five years in the same duplex on Morton Street, and she was sure that was everything Amber was going to need. She could be right after all: Amber needed a change, for sure, and she couldn't keep living in that apartment, the place that she had found, bought, renewed and decorated with Mike. He was everywhere in there. He was in the electric plugs that he had replaced by himself, especially the one in the bedroom that had apparently never worked before, but that he had somehow been able to fix. He was in the broken kitchen cabinet door that he had promised to repair by himself: he had never gotten the time to do so, and the door was still hanging from the cabinet, sadly crooked. He was in the business and finance books that were now accumulating dust on the living room shelves; he was in the only two novels he owned, forgotten presents that had never been opened: he didn't like reading stories about other people, he preferred to live his own life, instead. He was in the espionage movie DVDs and in the paintings they had bought during their vacations in Latin America. He was in the floors and in the walls, in the air and in each one of her breaths.

A man was waiting for them in front of the first building: - Rachel? - He asked Amber with a large smile.

She hated real estate people, especially in New York: most of them are like vampires, they suck all your blood and they leave you for dead in the street.

- I am Rachel - Her friend replied, shaking his hand before he could touch an already annoyed Amber.

- Nice to meet you Rachel, and who is your friend?

- She's the one looking for the apartment, but we'll choose together: she'll be fine - She answered with a wink.

The first apartment was a disaster, quite cheap but still a filthy disaster: Amber could never live there.

The second one was quite nice: a small one bedroom, third floor walk-up, could be decent after a deep enough cleaning.

- We'll take it - Rachel said.

- What? - Both Amber and the agent said at the same time.

- We'll take it - She repeated, and then whispered to Amber: - This is as good as it gets: you can't afford anything bigger in this area with your salary.

Amber tried to reply that she was fine with staying in her neighborhood and get twice the square feet with the same money, but Rachel's eyes were very clear: That's it. Amber had learned never to contradict those eyes. Never.

- Sure, we'll take it - Amber said in the end with a forged smile.

- We'll come by your agency tomorrow or Monday to sign the contract and leave you the deposit check - Rachel added, shaking the agent's hand.

- Thank you - Amber sighted a few minutes later while they were walking up on Bleecker Street, a GROM ice cream cup in her hand, Rachel's gluten-free muffin mysteriously forgotten at home.

- Don't thank me. Not for this: thank me because I'm not telling you that you shouldn't eat ice cream at ten in the morning. But at least you're eating something.

- Bacio is my favorite. And I'll give you the deposit back, as soon as I can.

- You don't have to thank me for that: I talked to your parents a couple of days ago, and they are more than happy to lend you the deposit money. I knew you'd appreciate if I took care of it directly with your mother.

Amber was very grateful for that: she hadn't seen her parents much after Mike's funeral, she didn't want them to see her so deeply stuck in that black hole of despair. Her parents had always been her pillars, and Mike's death had had an even stronger impact on them: they were not only mourning the loss of a young man they had learned to love very deeply, but they were also suffering for Amber's pain. She feared that double heartache could be too much for them, so she had preferred to keep her distance for a while.

- Thank you.

- I said don't thank me - Rachel had never been a very flexible person. All her exes said that was the reason why she didn't have a significant other... - At least not quite yet: you'll still need money. There's so much stuff you have to take care of: you have to hire someone to pack and move your things, rent a storage place to put the stuff you don't need, pay a rental agent to manage your apartment uptown...

- Wait, we have time for all these things, right? When will the rent start here?

- In two weeks.

- What? I'm not ready - Amber started to panic: she hadn't left her bed for two weeks, she couldn't even imagine the effort that an actual apartment move would require. She was definitely not ready to go in two weeks.

- I can't leave.

- Sure you can, but don't worry: I will help your parents take care of everything, you'll just have to go and relax.

- Go? - Amber was getting really confused.

- Yes, go. Take your plane, leave for your trip.

- My trip? What are you... - Then she understood what Rachel was talking about.

She looked at her friend, her eyes suddenly getting heavy, tired.

- You can't be thinking about that.

- Yes I can - Rachel said, simply.

- Rach, I can't go. I can't go on my own - It sounded so scary - I don't want to go on my own.

Rachel stopped walking and she put a hand on Amber's shoulder: - I'm not asking you if you want to go, I'm telling you that you will just go. Period. It's the only thing that makes sense now, and you owe it to Mike: he spent so much time planning for this trip. You told me that he organized everything, he booked all the resorts, he planned all the itinerary details. And now you don't want to go? You have already paid for everything!

- What do I care if it's paid?! - Amber raised her voice: she was loathing that conversation, and she was hating her friend for forcing her to discuss those things - He is dead, Rachel, if you hadn't noticed.

That was the first time that she heard the words in her own voice, and she couldn't stand them. They made her angry. Angry at Mike, Why did he have to die? Angry at her future, What will I do with my life? Angry at Rachel, Why don't you understand? Why don't you let me be?

Why didn't I die myself?

- I can't go! - She was yelling in the middle of the street.

- You can - Rachel put both her hands on Amber's shoulders and looked straight at her in the eyes - And it will help you, I promise: such a change of scenery will clean your mind and bring you peace. You'll think, you'll cry a bit, maybe, you'll meet nice people and see incredible things. You'll love it.

- Will I?! Will I love going alone on my honeymoon?!

ANNALISA CONTI

3 DARK TUNNEL

Mike had died almost exactly a month before their wedding.

Amber's mother had done all the hard work: she had canceled all reservations, paid all the fees, sent emails and letters to all the guests. The day of Mike's funeral Rachel had helped Amber's mother with the final touch: she had somehow sneaked the wedding dress out of Amber's apartment, and she had put it in her own closet. Rachel didn't know what to do with it, so she was just hiding it as long as it would take Amber to completely forget about it.

Amber kept thinking about the honeymoon, later that afternoon, and she was more and more convinced that it was just a bad idea. A horrible idea, the worst ever. Mike had planned everything, and he hadn't wanted her to know much about it: That's my present for you, my surprise, he had said.

He had planned everything to take her to more and more beautiful and heartwarming places, day after day, to surprise her with every activity and every resort, to make her dream at every sunrise and sunset. He had planned everything more than six months before, and she had accumulated so much expectation, so much excitement: they had been looking forward to it for such a long time, that she really couldn't wait to go. But not now, not anymore, not like this. Especially not on her own, not without him.

- I would kill myself, there on my own - She had told Rachel, who was sitting on Amber's sofa while looking at her friend: Amber was furiously pacing in her own living room, uncertain between rage, fear and despair.

- No you won't, it will be a breath of fresh air.

- I promise, I won't be able to survive this, I'm definitely not strong enough. I will take a full bottle of sleeping pills on the plane, or I will hang myself with a towel in the first hotel. I'm not kidding, I'm very serious - Amber looked at her friend right in the eyes: they both knew she wasn't joking.

- I know you're serious, I know you enough. That's why I will keep pushing you until I convince you that this is the best idea, the best thing you should do right now.

- I don't even know the details about anything: he booked all the hotels and stuff. And I don't even want to know: see, it was the point of the whole thing, me not knowing anything about it.

- Very well - Rachel looked at Amber with her half smile, her signature badass-lawyer half smile. Amber could picture Rachel flashing that smile in court while looking at the lawyer on the other side, every time she knew she was going to win the case. It was terrifying - Let's make a bet, then.

- No no no, you're too smart for me, you'll find a way to screw me anyway.

- Me? Never - The same smile, again - I want to be fair here, and let destiny decide for you. Are you in?

Rachel stretched out her hand, Amber was hesitant to take it: she knew her friend too well.

- I want to know the bet first - Amber said in the end.

- That's fair. I want to bet that Mike sent you calendar invites for every flight, hotel, activity, transfer that he had booked for your honeymoon. I want to bet that he also printed all documents and maybe already put them in the suitcase, ready to leave. If I'm right, you'll go, otherwise you'll stay.

- This is not fair, you know it. You know Mike is a consultant: he always has his plans perfectly organized and calendared.

- I sure know, he's a control freak! It's up to you: do you want to accept the bet, or are you a sissy?

Amber knew that she was going to lose that bet: Mike was a partner at McKinsey, a big business consulting firm, and everyone knew that he always had his stuff together. Not that Amber wouldn't have been able to plan a trip or organize an event on her own, but he was simply *better*.

- I'm not a sissy, anyway - She finally said with a sigh.

- There you go Amber! Now let me look at your phone calendar, and let's start packing.

Amber snorted, and gave her phone to Rachel.

Amber took the weekend off, and started to pack on the following Monday. She was not looking forward to it: her clothes were all mixed up with Mike's in the closet, in the laundry basket, and somehow both in the washer and in the dryer. That was the main reason why she hadn't left her pajama during the previous two weeks: she dreaded opening the closet and finding something that would make her scream again, or throw up, or both. Now she was still shaking at the idea of what she would find, but at least she had a reason to do it, she had a deadline: Rachel had promised her that she would come back on Friday night and Amber wanted her suitcase to be ready by then. She knew that her friend had the best intentions, but she was really scared by Rachel sometimes.

She opened the closet, and she immediately saw Mike's shirts: they were right there in the middle, fierce on their hangers, untouched in their laundry plastic wraps. A few of them were unwrapped, the weekend ones. All the way to the right of the colony, the blue one that he never wore: that was one of the first presents that Amber had offered him, years before. He had worn it twice: it didn't fit, but he hadn't wanted to change it or throw it away, so it just stayed there in the closet, almost new. Amber gave a hint of a smile: Mike had always been very practical, organized, linear, but sometimes with a pinch of unpredictability.

She was able to scroll the shirts all the way to the right hand side of the closet, and remove them from her sight with a sniffle; she randomly picked up and threw on her bed a few dresses that she wanted to bring with her. At least her jeans and t-shirts were all folded in her drawers, so she didn't have to skim through more of Mike's clothes to get to the majority of the things she would need.

Her underwear was in the nightstand's drawer, and she opened it carefully, since that was a small drawer and always too full of stuff. The first thing she saw, right on top of everything else, new and bright, was the white corset that she had bought for her wedding day. She carefully took it in her hands, she held it softly and she stared at it for a few very long seconds, petrified by a tsunami of memories: Mike and Amber picnicking in Central Park on a lazy Sunday afternoon, one summer long gone; Mike proposing to Amber with the ring on top of a chocolate cupcake, last year. Then some blurred pictures from faded dreams of the future: Amber telling Mike she was pregnant with their first child, a few months after their wedding; Mike and Amber celebrating Thanksgiving with her parents and their future kids. She couldn't bear the weight of all those dead hopes, of all those silver linings turned pitch black, and she fell on her knees with a puff, her body getting deflated and collapsing on itself. She was not ready for that. She was not ready for any of that. She closed her eyes and held on to the corset for a little longer; then suddenly she recognized it for what it was: a ghost from the past. She looked at it again and she screamed, in pain and anger. She threw the corset under the bed, swearing, shouting half words of despair. But no tears came out of her eyes: the drought was consuming her from the inside; she was slowly letting herself die.

She couldn't say for how long she had stayed there, motionless, sitting on her feet. Once the pain in her knees had become unbearable, she stood up, grasping the mattress not to fall down again, and she decided to just go to bed. She tossed on the floor all the clothes that she had selected from the closet, and she went under the blanket. Maybe she would try again tomorrow.

- What the hell happened here? - Friday night had come, and Rachel with it.

- I was not in the mood - Somehow she had also gotten back into her pajama.

Rachel hugged her and looked at her in the eyes: - Don't worry, I'm here now. Take a shower and I'll pack your stuff.

The shower helped: those tiny jets of water on her face had always had a liberating effect on Amber. Many opening paragraphs of her articles had come from there, many ideas and dreams. She felt like she didn't have any dreams anymore; maybe some ideas, all very dark, but still some ideas; definitely no paragraphs. She hadn't seen a movie in almost four weeks, which for her was like four years for a normal person: writing about movies was her job, and she loved it. At least, she used to: she felt she didn't care much about anything at that point.

- Are you still alive in there?

- I think so - Amber replied.

- Good, time to dry up. I'm done with packing.

Wow.

- I know, I'm awesome - Rachel replied with a wink.

Her packing skills were remarkable: everything was ready in Amber's suitcase, nicely folded. She had left some room for Amber's bath and beauty pieces, and included a soft bag to put souvenirs on the way back.

- I also printed your flight itineraries: you'll love it, you'll have so much time to watch movies, it will be perfect for you.

Amber tried to smile at her friend, but she was not sure if she was able to.

- So we have a New York City to Paris, Paris to Johannesburg, and Johannesburg to Windhoek. How does it sound?

- It sounds long and lonely. Can't you come with me?

- You know I can't: I can't take time off right now, surely not four weeks off.

- Not even for me? - Amber was thinking that everything could be so much easier for her if she didn't have to leave on her own, if she didn't have to face that trip by herself.

- You know I can't, sweetie - Rachel replied with a long hug.

- You work too much.

- Maybe, but I have the Lexington case to close. Which is just like the Fischer case back in 2008, but worse: the guy is actually guilty this time.

ANNALISA CONTI

4 THE WAY OUT

Kennedy airport, terminal 1, Amber was roaming the bookstores, to find something to read in case she had already seen all the movies on the plane: that happened so often. She saw the latest copy of Vanity Fair on the rack, she grabbed it and she slowly passed her hand on the cover with a strange weight in her chest: she quite missed her job, she missed the routine and the normality that her job had meant to her.

Every morning she used to wake up at six and do forty-five minutes of yoga at home, in the second bedroom. She was not very good at it, she had always been quite goofy, but yoga made her feel strong, it helped her get ready for the day and put her thoughts back into order after the night's sleep. Mike used to exercise with her in the morning, some pumps and some weight lifting to keep her company and laugh at her weird yoga music. That, if he wasn't travelling to one of the farthest corners of the world: he had always travelled a lot for his job, somehow he had always managed to get the crappiest projects in the crappiest places, so far away from New York to even require weekend travels sometimes. In those times she had hated his job with every piece of her being. The thing that made her the angriest was that she had never understood why Mike still liked the excitement of the roaming consulting life more than the happiness of a stable and regular existence. Sometimes she had felt she was never going to be enough for him, and that he was always going to need that adrenaline kick that he could only get from a straight 13-hour work session on a business class seat in a flight from New York to Dubai, drinking champagne and eating fresh salmon. The fact that he had died while coming back from one of those trips had only made her even angrier.

Amber used to get to her office every morning by 7:30 am, to catch up with the European newspapers and the late night news from the West Coast, keeping an eye on her agenda for any early morning commitments. She was an entertainment journalist, a movie nerd, as Mike would usually put it: she covered mostly cinema, and some TV, the "quality TV" as she would call it, or more simply HBO. Every year she got to go to several film festivals in the US and in Europe: that was her favorite side of her job. Actually, she used to love every side of her job: she was paid to go to the movie theater, she couldn't think about anything smarter to do for a living. Now it was the beginning of May, and she was going to miss Cannes that year.

They had been very understanding at work, telling her to take all the time that she needed: two months, three months, even more. She could send something from time to time, if she felt like writing a few lines, or even no lines at all, that wasn't going to be a problem. In the previous month she hadn't sent anything, she hadn't even opened her computer: she had felt so dry in the inside that she hadn't even been able to think about work. She had decided to take her laptop with her to Africa, but she didn't even know why.

She paid for her copy of Vanity Fair at the counter, and she flipped through it while waiting to board.

It all went by quite fast: sleep, read, watch a movie; French customs, wait, board; sleep, read, watch a movie; South African customs, wait, get a burger, board; look outside the window, sleep, look more outside the window; Namibian customs, breath.

What time was it now? Who knew. Amber felt lost, so far from everything and everyone she knew, in the wrong time zone, even in the wrong hemisphere, so *alone*. That feeling made her shiver: for the first time she was realizing how truly alone she was now. She wondered how her new life would look like: home delivery dinners for one, always ordering too much food not to have to pay for the delivery service; going to the movies for leisure by herself, watching out for the pervs and weirdos she had always feared in the darkness of a movie theater; going out with friends and being the only single person in a land of couples. She was surprised to realize how many consequences Mike's death was going to have on her life, so many practical effects she hadn't even started to consider. Amber suddenly felt horrible for being so material about it, for giving importance to all those tiny details that would never diminish the fact that her life had no meaning and no purpose, now that he was gone. That was the only consequence that mattered.

She walked in the airport for what looked like a very long time, her loneliness getting even amplified by the numerous couple and family reunions that seemed to surround her. Everyone was happy to be there: kids were flying in their parents' arms, friends were screaming at each other with laughter, husbands were carrying flowers for their wives. Everyone was happy to be there, everyone except for her: she was falling at the bottom of her infinite misery, and she would have paid all the money in the world *not* to be there in that moment.

Amber sighed in slight relief when she finally saw a familiar sign: AVIS. For sure they would know what time it was, and they should also have a car waiting for her.

- Hey I have a reservation, I printed my papers, the name is Stevens - She said almost without breathing, anxiously showing the papers to the employee.

- Good afternoon, Miss Stevens. You said Stevens, right? - The employee started to go through the pile of documents he had on his desk - Unfortunately I can't find a reservation at this name. Maybe it was made under another last name?

- You're right, the name should be Gillingham - She said after a second, and that made her regret having left New York even more than ever: why was she there? Nothing was right anymore, not even her name. Why wasn't Mike with her? Why did she have to do that without him? Nothing made sense.

- What time is it? - She added at the end, with a deep sigh.

- There you are Miss Gillingham, I found your reservation! It is 1:30 pm, welcome to Namibia - The man added with a large smile - Your car is ready outside.

She was relieved: she didn't know anything about the trip, she had just hoped that all the details in Mike's calendar invites, and everything he had printed, were final, and that nothing had changed in the meantime. At least the car was there.

- I just need your driver's license and your credit card - The AVIS employee explained her, while printing her contract on an old dot matrix printer - And a few signatures here, here, and here - He concluded, scribbling small crosses where she had to sign.

- Do you want the additional tire insurance? - He asked her in the end.

- Tire insurance?

- Yes Miss, in case you get a flat tire: with this insurance someone can come to help you.

- And this is not already included, right?

- No Miss, you have to pay additional ten dollars per day if you want it.

- I think I'm fine - She replied in the end: if Mike had decided not to get it, there must have been a reason; for sure he had considered it and thought they didn't need it. She would trust him on that.

- Very well Miss. Do you want the additional accident insurance?

- I think I'm fine - She repeated, with a perplexed look on her face and hoping that everything would actually be fine.

- Very well Miss - He smiled back - You can take your keys and you will find the car outside, number 43. Do you need help? Oh I see you only have a small bag, but let me know if I can help you with it.

The car was a big SUV, a huge thing, but the AVIS employee had insisted on the fact that it was not a four wheel drive, so she shouldn't drive it outside of the official roads, especially not on soft sand. That was one of the very few things that Mike had told her about their trip: he had needed to rent a car in Namibia with a return in Botswana, and AVIS was the only company that would allow that. For some reasons, though, they wouldn't allow a Jeep or any other 4WD to be picked up and dropped off in two different African countries, so he had done the best he had been able to.

He should have probably told her something else about the car, because she had quite an unexpected surprise: she placed her luggage on the back seat, she entered the car, she seated on the front left seat, and she didn't find the wheel in front of her.

- What the…? - She shouted out loud.

Mike had forgotten to tell her that in Namibia they drive on the opposite side of the road, like in the United Kingdom: Namibia had been colonized by both the English and the Germans through the years, but that amazing British heritage had somehow gotten stuck there. That explained why the wheel was not where it was supposed to be on the dashboard.

One more thing was wrong there, and she wondered how many more she was going to face during that damned trip. She mouthed a curse word, she turned around the car, and she thanked Mike for having rented an automatic car: she would have never been able to change gears with her left hand. To be honest, she was not sure she could have managed it with her right hand, either.

The parking guys insisted to give her maps of Namibia, a pretty remarkable pile of maps of the country's different regions. She was not sure she needed them: Mike had printed maps and itineraries from Google Maps, and she always had her phone to do a few seconds of roaming and GPS in case she got lost. Right.

Amber quite soon discovered that Namibia is not a very GPS-friendly country. The airport was on the eastern side of Windhoek, the capital city, and she needed to go all the way down south-west to reach her first destination: a lodge in the middle of the Kalahari Desert, a vast desert region located in the center-south area of the country. Google Maps led her towards downtown Windhoek, on the only road that goes east-west in that area, the B6. Crossing the city was another story: she followed the printed instructions, passing by schools dedicated to German personalities, buildings with Dutch names and Afrikaans neighborhoods. She drove by Castro Street and Mugabe Avenue, getting surprised by the fact that a free country like

Namibia had named an avenue after Robert Mugabe, the very much controversial President of Zimbabwe.

Soon enough, she got stuck in an impasse.

She was not used to getting lost: she didn't drive much, since she lived in New York City, but every time she had gone somewhere with Mike she had always been an excellent navigator. She checked the printed maps again, and she understood the issue: where Google Maps was saying she should turn left, there was no left turn anymore. They seemed to have recently redone the tarmac there, and they must have somehow decided to just keep going straight, and build a sidewalk where before there was a left turn. Somehow she managed not to panic. She took her phone out of her backpack, she turned it on and she waited for something to happen on the upper left corner of the screen, where the network symbols are. She waited for the daunting "Searching..." to turn into the Namibian equivalent of AT&T, but instead an even more frightening "No Service" appeared.

Now she felt it was her right to panic, and she panicked.

She was completely alone on the other side of the world, where she didn't know anything, she didn't seem to understand anything, and everything seemed to have one purpose: confusing her and making her feel miserable. She started to bump her head against the wheel.

- Rachel, why in hell did I let you convince me to do this? - She yelled, mostly at herself.

Her brain finally rebooted after a few seconds, and she could recall a very important detail: she had the map. Somehow she found out where she was and what way she should follow to get out of town, and she restarted the car: it was complicated to drive and look at the map at the same time, but she was more than willing to just go with it.

- Mike, you should drive here - She snorted out loud to keep herself company, once again trying to remember why was she there and what was she exactly doing there, and once again not finding any decent answers to her questions.

Somehow she managed to find the entrance to the B1, the main Namibian highway that runs north-south across the country; she now had to drive on it for a bit more than two hours, and she would get to her lodge.

She wanted to get there as soon as she could: she was tired, and sick of travelling. She couldn't wait for that dreadful first part of her trip to be over as soon as possible, and she especially wanted to reach a comfortable and nice hotel where she could get some rest, and feel a bit less miserable for about two minutes, the time of a hot shower. Also, Mike had booked some activity at six pm, an unspecified "sundowner", and she wanted to honor his memory and get the best out of it.

And then she saw them on the side of the road and she couldn't keep it together: she had to stop the car; she stared at them long enough to finally remember about her camera, and take a picture. Two baboons were quietly walking down the highway, pausing from time to time to sniff the air, pick up something to eat from the grass, look around. They were beautiful, goofy but beautiful. She had been to the zoo several times, so those were not the first baboons that she had ever seen in her life, but there was something different in them: they were free. Their eyes could look around and roam the savannah, all around them; animals in zoos have all the same sad eyes, the eyes of someone who was born in a zoo, who has never seen the savannah or the desert, doesn't even know they exist, but still somehow feels that something is missing, that there's a hole somewhere inside of her. Amber had been feeling just the same since she had lost Mike; what was worse, she knew exactly how big the hole was in her chest, and how fast it was devouring her from the inside.

She had to stop a second time to take another picture further down the road, when she saw a big sign: Tropic of Capricorn.

She had always loved taking pictures of signs: from "Welcome to Virginia" to "Yellowstone National Park" and "Roma", she loved mementos, pictures of places where she and Mike had been, that she used to post on their fridge. Her biggest fear was to forget, to wake up one day empty, realizing she didn't remember who she was, who Mike was, the things she had done with him in her life, the happiness they had shared. She had thought that their kids would have helped her: just by looking at them, they would have reminded her of the life that she and Mike would have lived together, of the people they would have become and of the wonderful children they would have raised. That idea hit her in the stomach, out of nowhere: that life was gone, that possibility of the future had disappeared. There were no kids, there were never going to be. They were gone, with Mike.

She had to sit down in the dirt, her back leaning against the car, still looking at the Tropic of Capricorn sign. She couldn't breathe, she couldn't think. And she still couldn't cry either, so she kept panting and cursing Mike's death for several minutes.

The only thing she was able to think about, for some strange reason, was that scene from Back To The Future Part Two, when Marty comes back from 2015 to 1985. Only he arrives to an altered 1985, where everything is wrong: his father is dead, his mother is married to Biff, and Doc is in a mental hospital. Everything that he knew and had is gone; his future, as well as the present he used to live in, is gone. Amber wished she had a time machine to save Mike, just like Marty was able to bring everything back to normal.

- I guess there's no Doc here, there's no Delorean, there's no turning back: this is the only possible present, and there's no solution to this misery.

She stood up as suddenly as she had collapsed, she got back into the car and she resumed her drive. She didn't say a word, she stopped the music, she kept looking straight in front of her. Her brain and her heart were blank spaces.

She had seen a few signs for the Kalahari Dunes Lodge in the previous ten miles, so she was ready to turn right in the dirt road when she finally saw the arrow sign. A few minutes later she saw a majestic gate, with the name of the lodge carved on it and two giant giraffe statues on its two sides. Remove the giraffes, imagine two triceratops just past the gate, and you will have the entrance to Jurassic Park.

There didn't seem to be any dinosaurs or other dangerous animals around her, so she felt safe enough to exit her car, open the gate to let her SUV in, drive through the gate and close it behind her shoulders. The dirt road was going to continue for a couple more miles, according to the small sign that she saw on her left.

The gate was the only break in the electrified fence. She found it quite interesting: she had seen similar fences around many nice houses in the center of Windhoek. She wondered who were the most dangerous animals that Namibians had to protect themselves from: lions or humans?

5 A DESERT OF DREAMS

The lodge was much more than she had expected. She knew that each place was going to be unique and wonderful, and that Mike had planned the trip to be a crescendo of emotions and beauty, from the first place to the last one. If that was the first one, she couldn't even imagine what to expect next.

The reception was a lonely wooden building in the middle of a sea of yellow grass, connected to the main parking, where she had temporarily left her car, by a wooden boardwalk. She had followed the "reception" arrow, and enjoyed walking in the sun: spring hadn't fully reached New York yet, when she had left, and she was craving for some warmth. Once inside, a tall man came towards her:

- Good afternoon Miss, welcome to the Kalahari Dune Lodge. My name is Tungue, but you can call me Tom.

- Hi Tom, my name is Amber, nice to meet you.

- Amber, you come from the trees, and you're solid, strong. It's good to have you here - Tungue continued with a smile, and he walked behind the wooden counter to offer her a drink - This is our special welcome drink, to soothe your thirst.

The drink was cold and sweet, her chest felt immediately a bit lighter. Surely she didn't feel solid or strong at all.

- May I ask you under what name is your reservation, Miss Amber?

- It should be Gillingham - She answered with a sigh. She hated to say that name out loud, she hated the sound of it in her American accent: she missed the way Mike used to pronounce it, "the correct way", as he would say, with his perfect Oxford pronunciation.

- There you are, shall I assume that your husband is in the car?

- Oh, no. I'm on my own actually.

Tungue looked at her with an uncertain smile and a question in his eyes.

- Yes, actually - Amber's head suddenly felt light, as it did each time she had no idea of what to do. And as it usually happened, her mouth started to produce words without first getting connected to her brain - Mr. Gillingham is my… my assistant, he booked the trip for me, but I'm here on my own.

- I see. The reservation is for two people, though.

- Hehe - At that point her brain took control again, but it was too late: her subconscious attempt to look modern and cool was already failing - Yes, I always tell my assistant to book rooms for two people, they're usually bigger and nicer.

She tried a smile: - Sometimes he even says that the two people travelling are a couple on honeymoon, to get me an even nicer room. Hehe he is a very nice assistant - She now felt really stupid - You know, I travel a lot: I'm a journalist, I'm writing a series of travel articles on this area of Africa.

She thought she was now sounding more convincing, but she still doubted. She couldn't tell where that lie about why she was on her own had come from. Better: she was not sure why Mike had to become her assistant, but she knew that she didn't want to talk about the true reason, she didn't want to *explain* it. She couldn't stop thinking about Mike, but she didn't want to talk about him, to mention his name and describe who he was to other people: she was jealous of her memories of him. In addition to that, she was sick of being pitied by people and seeing that sad and compassionate look on their faces. She had already glimpsed it so many times, and it could never hide what they were really thinking: I hope this does never happen to me.

Tungue looked at her again, more perplexed: - I see. This is your key - He then added, handing her a key with a big wooden keychain with the number 12 on it.

- We gave you the last cabin, there's more privacy. You want privacy if you're a couple on honeymoon, right? You can take your car and follow the arrows to reach your cabin; I'll meet you there to help you with your luggage.

The cabin had a beautiful patio with an unblocked view of the savannah, with its burned grass, bushes and some rare trees. Tungue opened the door on a giant bed and a restroom with an open shower.

- I will be your guide for the sundowner that your assistant booked for you. We will meet at the reception at six pm. You may want to bring a jacket: the air freshens up when the sun goes down - He added in the end, looking at her shirt.

- Is there a Wi-Fi anywhere?

She had gone back to the reception a few minutes before six; she had looked for some kind of network in her room but she hadn't found any. Not that she needed it: she had texted both her mom and Rachel when she had landed in Windhoek, and she wasn't expecting anything from anyone. That had been so strange to realize that she didn't have anyone else, nobody else she wanted to stay in touch with. But she just wasn't used not to be connected, to be left outside of the world, without news. She realized that most likely she wasn't going to find Wi-Fi in many places: that was going to be a great rehab for her!

- Never mind - She added with a hand gesture, and she got ready to follow Tungue wherever he wanted to take her.

- You can wait for Tungue in the car - The lady employee told her - It will be the big open jeep in the parking, a couple of people should already be on board.

Safaris would take place either early in the morning or later in the afternoon, when animals would be more active to look for food, be it grass or a tastier piece of meat; the sundowner was a safari at sunset, when the sky and the grass melt in each other in the greens and yellows of the savannah.

42

A couple in their fifties was already in the car, a camera around her neck and a binocular in his hands. She sat behind them.

- Hello, I'm Jackie and this is my husband David, how are you?

- Hi, I'm Amber, nice to meet you.

- Oh you're from the US! - The woman kept talking, showing a larger smile as soon as she glimpsed Amber's accent - We live in Toronto, Canada, where are you from?

- I live in New York - Amber replied with a polite smile. She loved Canadian people: they have the worst winters, yet they never complain, they just keep going, they keep smiling while shoveling tons of snow and walking underground to go to work. She thought about all the articles and blog posts about New York's seasonal inconveniences that come out every winter: New Yorkers should all go to Canada for winter survival trainings. They would stop complaining. Amber almost grinned.

- Are you here on vacation? - David asked.

- No, I'm actually here for work: I'm a journalist and I'm writing a series of articles on this area of Africa - The lie had already started to grow in her, like a dream of living someone else's life - I write for the National Geographic.

- Oh this is fascinating! Are you also a photographer? - Jackie kept asking - Oh you must be, you must have a great camera in that backpack. I am a bit of a photography lover myself: David and I planned this trip for our thirtieth wedding anniversary, and he also offered me this camera. He said I needed something great for Africa.

Jackie looked at David with dreamy eyes, and Amber couldn't stop herself from being jealous: she would never grow old with Mike. She would never count the wrinkles on his face, she would never lean against him while walking up a step. She couldn't tell if she was feeling more angry or desperate at that point.

Luckily, Tungue had jumped in the car and started the engine, so that the couple turned their backs on Amber to look at their safari guide, and Amber could hide her grieving eyes behind her sunglasses.

The car was just starting to move, when Tungue warned them that they were going to see zebras and gazelles that day, and maybe a giraffe if they were lucky, but no predators: the lodge was built inside a private reserve, where animals were protected not only from cats but also from poachers, the two most dangerous species of predators that could still be found in Africa.

- Is poaching a big problem here? - Amber's interest was sincere, not driven by her fake National Geographic article.

- Here in the reserve things are fine - Tungue replied - Because we don't have rhinos or elephants: poachers are mostly interested in tusks and horns, and our springboks and zebras are not very appealing.

- Do you mean that poachers still kill rhinos for their horns?

- Yes Miss Amber, demand is still very high: people in China and other parts of Asia still believe in their medicinal and aphrodisiac effects, so local poachers still make money with killing rhinos - Tungue turned his head towards the back of the car to look at her for a second, then he turned it back straight to pay attention to the road - You are

44

American, you should know it: business is business, and where there's demand there's always offer.

He was right, but that idea of killing wild animals for money was too far from her world and culture for her to fully grasp it. Many species were endangered in Africa, she was pretty sure that rhinos were a protected species. Yet, the idea of killing them for a few immediate hundred bucks (or whatever the price of a horn was) still sounded appealing to some people, more than preserving them as long as possible to keep attracting tourists from all over the world to see them. Certainly, zoos also remove animals from their natural habitats and they put them in cages where they cannot move, let alone run free for miles in the savannah. But at least they are alive. They are not hunted, they are fed, but freedom is the price they pay. Amber was not sure if that was still worth being called life: what's life without freedom for a wild animal?

Too much thinking for me, she thought. She grabbed her camera from her backpack, and she started to take pictures to keep her mind busy with something else.

- On our left, a group of springboks, the animals I was telling you about - Tungue was yelling to get heard on top of the car noise, and Amber could capture the springboks with her zoom: they looked like small gazelles, with orange-brown backs, white bellies and cute snouts - I hope you can see them run: they are so light and elegant when they jump in the grass.

Further down the road they crossed a group of zebras; they were quietly walking around in the warm sunlight, and they didn't seem at all scared by the car.

- They don't know what we are - Tungue was explaining - But they can feel we are not a danger for them: we don't have fangs or nails, and we make so much noise that we could never be a predator, we would starve!

They also saw a lonely gnu walking in the tall grass: she stared at the car for a few seconds, fierce with her pointy horns and her brave black face, then she shook her tail and she kept walking.

It was time to stop for refreshments, so Tungue drove them up to a very scenic spot, from where they could take pictures of the sunset. Its beauty was stunning. Long shadows were melting in the grass, and the sky was a rainbow of reds and oranges to the west, with purples and blues coming from the east. An ostrich was running towards the sun not too far from them, her tail feathers voluptuously following the wind, her long neck elegantly flowing at each step. Amber wished she could run towards a brighter tomorrow like that beautiful bird, a bird that can't fly with wings but can float in the wind. She saw a couple of kudus on her right, in the distance: bigger versions of the springboks, but completely brown, the two female kudus were walking in and out of the shades, going home before it got too dark outside. They stopped from time to time, the first one looked around, she attuned her ears to spot troubles, then she kept going. Amber was so focused on them that she almost didn't hear Tungue screaming:

- ... If we hurry we can reach them before night comes, let's go!

They reached the giraffes a few minutes later. There were

only four giraffes in the reserve, and all four of them were walking together in the last light of the day, hurrying to reach something: water, a safer place, home. Tungue explained that they usually spent most of their days together: giraffes are very social and extremely loyal to each other. They were beautiful with their long legs, and they had that unique way of smoothly moving their heads up and down with their long necks while they were walking. Their eyes kept looking at Amber and the other people while they were crossing the road in front of the car, and Amber felt captured by those sweet sad eyes. For a moment she almost forgot her own sadness, lost in that silky gaze. She zoomed with her camera on their faces, and she saw some sort of awareness behind those long eyelashes: the beauty of freedom, the smell of the savannah, the soft noises in the sunset.

6 DEAD RIVER

Dinner had been plentiful and delicious the night before, with lamb stew and berry pie, but Amber was famished when she woke up the following day. She had dreamed about the starry sky of Namibia, where nothing was in the right place, and all constellations were new to her. In her dream she had been an astronaut lost in space, a lone pilgrim that had been sucked in a black hole and was now long forgotten by anybody on Earth. Tungue had tried to teach her a few names of constellations the previous night, but the Southern Cross was the only one she could remember now - maybe she had already heard or read about it, in a book or in a movie.

Breakfast was huge and quick: she wanted to leave early for her next destination.

- You're already leaving, Miss Amber - Tungue was finalizing her check out, while holding on his usual large smile - But you're right: Namibia is a beautiful country, there are so many things to see. I hope you had a good time here in the Kalahari Desert, and that you'll find what you're looking for… And your article, of course, it will be a success! Where are you going from here?

- I want to visit Mariental, the guide book says it's a nice typical village, and then I'll go to Sossusvlei.

Sossusvlei was all the way to the west, separated from the ocean by a thick desert of sand and dunes.

- Oh I don't think you'll have time for Mariental - Tungue looked at his watch and then back at Amber - And there is not much to see there. You should go straight to Sossusvlei: take the B1 north, turn left on the C21 and then you just keep going, you can't miss it.

Amber was perplexed: - Are you sure? Google Maps says it will take me six hours if I pass by Mariental, and it's not even 8 am…

Tungue was amused: - Oh Miss Amber, you shouldn't trust Google Maps so much here in Namibia! But trust me instead, and go straight to Sossusvlei: it will take you all day to get there. Remember the sun goes down early in this season: it's winter here.

Amber looked at him and she decided, though not fully convinced, to listen to him.

Needless to say, Tungue was right. Well, Google Maps was also technically right: the software calculates travel times based on speed limits, then it corrects for traffic. If traffic is not an issue in Namibia, at least outside of Windhoek, the speed limit isn't always a good proxy of the speed at which a car would be able to run on the road...

Amber left the lodge and she drove north on the B1; that was the main north-south arterial road in the country, and the tarmac looked new and almost impeccable. When she turned left on the C21, as Google Maps wanted her to and as Tungue had confirmed, she found a less nice but still very decent concrete road, where the speed limit panel said 100 km/hour. Amber had to do the calculation in her mind to realize that it was some 60 miles/hour: definitely quite high for a concrete road. After a mile, concrete turned into raw gravel and she had to slow down considerably. She was still quite confident, though: it was going to be like that only for a few feet, maybe they were just redoing that portion of the road.

It wasn't only for a few feet, and nobody was working on that portion: all secondary ways in Namibia are gravel roads, no exceptions. Speed limits are between 60 and 100 km/hour, some 40 and 60 miles/hour, but it is still gravel. Everywhere.

At that point she understood why the AVIS employee had offered her the additional tire insurance, and she deeply regretted not taking it: it seemed a much needed add-on now. She suddenly got very worried: what if anything happened? How would she call for help in the middle of the desert? How would she survive by herself? She felt very small and very stupid for having taken that long road by herself. She then grinned when she realized that Mike must have had no idea about the road conditions in Namibia, either, or he would have included that additional safety level in their trip, and purchased the tire insurance. Nobody is infallible after all, not even Mike.

She also soon realized that she had almost two hundred miles in front of her, at twenty-five or thirty miles per hour. She mouthed a thank to Tungue, she added a curse, and then she turned up the volume of her iPhone: luckily, she had enough offline songs on her playlist to fill those seven to eight hours of driving.

Grasslands, dunes, and mountains went by, with the landscape slowly and constantly evolving from one to the other. The sky was untouched by clouds, the air calm, the sun bright, Amber was mostly alone on the road; the few cars that she crossed would leave thick clouds of dust behind them, that would hang in the air for a long time.

Amber stopped at the first town she encountered, after having passed a few villages: as the AVIS employee had told her at the airport, gas and cash were the two things she had to be sure always to have plenty of in Namibia. She had decided to totally follow all instructions and advices she had received, to try not to give herself any additional reasons to panic. There were not many gas stations outside of Windhoek, so she had to be very diligent and refill every time she had the chance to do it. Also, credit cards were not accepted everywhere, and banks didn't always have cash in their ATMs, so money was the second most important thing to keep an eye on. To avoid any risk, at the airport Amber had taken plenty of dollars, widely accepted across all Southern African countries: a stronger currency, less prone to inflation. Mike had told her that, for example, in Zimbabwe the inflation had been so bad, at some point during the civil war, that money had kept losing value from one day to the next one, and the country had started to coin one hundred million Zimbabwean dollar bills. Some of those bills still existed, and they were sold to tourists as a souvenir, for a few US dollars.

Amber was eating an ice-cream at the gas station, the tank refilled, smiling at the memory of Mike's passion for economics and politics: he had been so full of interests. She had always loved the way they had perfectly completed each other: they were very different, but they had always been able to appreciate and leverage their disparities, and that had made their couple stronger and stronger. But that was also why the dissolution of that couple had been so incredibly painful for Amber: she had lost the main part of her own self, the part that completed her love for sciences with a deep understanding of economics, that matched her need for novels and stories with a craving for documentaries, that balanced her jokes with captivating conversations. She had never felt so disconnected from her own self.

Later in the afternoon, Amber reached Sesriem, a very small village built at the entrance gate of the Namib National Park, in the Namib Desert. Sossusvlei is the heart of the desert and of the National Park, and it is a spectacular dry dead marsh. The Sossusvlei basin once in a while is filled by the water of the Tsauchab, the seasonal river that contributed to the creation of the basin, thousands of years ago. Mike had booked the only lodge located inside the park for their three-night stay: according to the travel guides and websites that he had been studying for a long time to prepare for the trip, the most spectacular activity to do in the park is watching the sunrise from the red sand dunes that surround Sossusvlei. Since the park opens at dawn and Sossusvlei is almost forty miles from the entrance, the only way to be on top of a dune at sunrise is to sleep in the park, and get ready to wake up around four am. She was ready: This is not a vacation, she was telling herself, This trip has to have a meaning, for me and for Mike, and for everything he meant to me.

The lodge was a few miles past the park entrance gate, and she could see it approaching from the road: a small sparse group of wooden cabins, with roofs made of black canes, and a bigger service building in the middle. The edifices looked like stones in the desert, almost hidden to conceal the presence of human beings in the National Park.

- Welcome to Sossusvlei Lodge - A hand waving and a smile greeted her at the parking area - You can leave your car here and follow me to the reception.

Amber smiled back to the young girl, and followed her on the gravel and sand path.

- Unfortunately your room is not ready yet - Minda, that was the name of the girl, was telling Amber - I am very sorry for this, but you can leave your bags here, maybe visit something here in the park, and come back in one hour or so.

Amber was surprised, since it was past 4:30 pm, but she was happy to get something out of that day, other than driving and driving, and then driving again. She was not sure where to go, though.

- You can visit the Sesriem Canyon - Minda replied to Amber's silent question - It's very close to the lodge, only a few minutes driving, and it is very beautiful and unique.

Minda was showing her a map of the area, while she kept talking about the canyon: - It was created by the Tsauchab River thousands of years ago, just like the whole Sossusvlei area, and it is made of beautiful rocks. Around sunset it becomes even more beautiful: the rocks take the orange and red colors of the sun, and looking at the sky's changing nuances from inside the canyon is an unforgettable emotion.

Amber was soon convinced, and she later told Minda that the canyon was absolutely worth the trip: not only the rocks had a million different shades of orange and red at sunset, but the shapes of the canyon itself, with its arches and narrow passages, its caves and its subterranean ponds, were impressive. She had been to the Grand Canyon a long time before, and she remembered it as a spectacular place: vast when seen from the top, suffocating when walking or canoeing at its bottom, the Grand Canyon had given her a sense of bewilderment. She had felt so small and so insignificant if compared to the canyon's life cycle, like a fruit fly that you barely notice, and it is gone before you can actually see it. The Sesriem Canyon had been a deeper and more touching experience for her: in some points the canyon was so narrow that she could touch its walls, she could feel the millennia that had passed by there, the action of wind and water, unmodified by humans. She had found it so liberating: something men hadn't wrecked, yet, something still living its life as it was supposed to be. She wished she could say the same thing about herself.

She was still in a very open-hearted mood when she came back to the lodge and entered her cabin; her luggage was waiting for her in the middle of a large open space occupied by a poster bed on her right and an open washroom on her left. She had learned in the Kalahari Desert why poster beds were so common everywhere in Namibia: bugs. Maybe that was not their season, since it was winter, but many things had been flying around at night, and she was very happy about her Malarone prophylaxis against malaria, just in case. The wooden walls of the cabin were very warm and rustic, and the window wall in front of her invited her to walk outside on the terrace: the view on the Namib Desert was incomparable.

She glanced something on the far left of the terrace, and she understood why the staff had needed more time to get her room done: there were two cane armchairs, with a small table in front of them and an empty wine bucket on the table. Mike must have booked another honeymoon suite, she pondered, but when Amber had arrived to the lodge by herself Minda must have understood that something was off. Most likely Minda had asked the housekeepers to remove the honeymoon installation (Flowers? Fruits? Wine?), and the wine bucket had just been forgotten on the terrace. Minda had done everything Amber needed: ask no questions, not to force her to think about it one more time, not to make her strained loneliness become even heavier on her shoulders and on her heart. She fought not to let her depression chase away the peaceful feelings she had picked up in the canyon; she was not sure if she was going to win her battle against herself.

Amber was ready for dinner a few minutes in advance, so she decided to have a drink in the lounge, before paying her visit to the restaurant terrace. The lounge had a Wi-Fi connection, and for the first time in two days Amber downloaded her emails. The only message she opened was from Rachel, mainly because the subject said "Open and be excited":

"Amber!

I know you're loving your trip and thanking me every minute for having convinced you to move your fat ass and go - so ok, you're welcome.

I'll be quick: everything is done. Your new apartment is ready for you when you come back: as your mom and I had agreed (and now that I think about it I'm not really sure if we ever actually discussed it with you), she hired some great movers (you should have seen them, those biceps…) who brought to the new flat all the furniture that we were able to fit in there. Not much to be honest: the new place is small, but it will be great for you. Everything else is in storage, don't worry about it. We also moved your stuff, of course, your clothes and shoes (I might - I'm not saying that I did, but I might - have accidentally slipped a couple of dresses in my bag and brought them home with me), and I tried to maintain your order, more or less. You will see for yourself once you're back. Trust me: the apartment is gorgeous, see pics attached!

That's all, you'll love it.
I love you dear,
R "

Amber had to admit it: the pictures in the attachment showed a gorgeous apartment, a place that she didn't know yet but somehow already contained all her things. Her paintings and movie posters were already on the walls, and she could also spot some pictures of her and Mike: once hanging in their bedroom, they were now sitting on top of a console in the living room. She was glad Rachel had kept them, instead of putting them away in storage.

She didn't know if she was ever going to feel at home in any place that was not their apartment, with anyone that was not Mike. She didn't know if she could ever be herself again with another person, as she was with him: he had seen all of her, and he had somehow been able to love it all. Who else could do it?, she asked herself, And who else ever could I love? That thought scared her and paralyzed her for a while.

She finished her drink with a long sip, she shook her head to toss all those unwanted thoughts far away from her brain, and she went to dinner: she didn't want to think about the future, not now, not that night.

7 DAWN

Sunrise. A simple thing that happens every day, everywhere in the world. Yet, that one had been ravishing.

The alarm went on at four am, but Amber was already awake, sleepless in a strange excitement for what she knew was going to be a very special event: the sunrise over Sossusvlei's dunes was the only detail Mike had mentioned to her about their trip, the one thing he had seemed to care about the most, and for which he had made special arrangements. He had booked a private jeep driver (with an actual four wheel drive car) to bring them to Big Daddy, the highest dune in Sossusvlei, to watch the sun rising from its top.

The car ride was lonely, the driver didn't speak much, and Amber imagined strange wild beasts attacking them in the darkness. After one hour she was ready to jump out of the car and breathe the fresh air.

- That is Big daddy, behind that other smaller dune - The driver was showing her the way - Can you see where those other people are climbing? You better hurry: the sun will start rising above the mountains in a few minutes, and you want to be on top of Big Daddy with your camera ready when it starts!

Amber started to run: she didn't want to miss it.

She didn't know how difficult it is to climb a sand dune as grand as Big Daddy, which is almost a thousand feet high. Reaching its feet was not too complicated, even if her mountain shoes were heavy and sank in the soft red sand, but she was already out of breath when she started to climb. Dunes are tricky: you have to walk right on the edge to avoid slipping on either side, and you have to walk slowly and steadily not to move the sand around too much. Amber had to be very careful, and she tried to follow the footsteps left by the small group of people that were climbing their way up a couple of hundred feet in front of her. Her heart was bouncing in her chest, while she was pacing as fast as she could.

She wanted to honor Mike's memory by capturing the first beam of sunlight of that day, with her eyes and with her camera. She wanted to let him know that she was doing all that for him, she wanted to show him that she was still and forever there for him, because he still was the most important thing in her life, and he would always be, even if he was gone. She could see him standing there, waiting for her on the highest crest of the dune, a few steps away. He was smiling at her, while encouraging her with that accent of his, mostly perfectly British but with a bit of something else, a mix of cultures and bloods. He had wanted to go to Africa for their honeymoon to honor the continent where his mother was born, and that Nigeria that she had left decades before for a new life in London, never to go back. Nigeria itself was not an ideal place for a honeymoon, though, therefore Mike had in the end picked Southern Africa. Even if his roots had been calling him to Africa for a long time, he had never been there; he had sometimes considered moving there, but it had always been nothing more than an idea, almost a joke: I am an Englishman, I need temperate weather and an umbrella in my computer bag, he used to say. For sure he had found enough rain in New York City, where McKinsey had transferred him from London several years before.

She could see him there, tall and elegant like the first time she had met him, the same sly smile he had had at that Vanity Fair event. Condé Nast had been his client at the time, and he had been invited to some party during the Tribeca Film Festival in New York, a few years before. Somehow Mike's tuxedo and Amber's gown were the exact same shade of blue, that night, and he had approached her with the lamest move she had ever heard in her life: "I'm glad you got my message and picked the right color". "What a jerk", she had thought, just before looking at him and hopelessly falling in love with him. It still made her smile.

Mike was waiting for her on top of the dune, with a khaki jacket and a backpack, one hand thrown out towards her to help her reach him, his eyes shining like gems. She had lost herself a million times in those eyes, and she had been longing for them with her whole body. She wanted to carve that picture of Mike deeper and deeper in her heart.

She squinted her eyes in the rising light, and she was finally able to see the truth in front of her: that wasn't Mike. The guy was just part of the group of people that preceded her, and that she had now just joined.

The sun started to come out. There were a few clouds right around it, and the sunrise that morning was an explosion of warmth and color: a bright orange sky was suddenly illuminating the dunes, chasing the shades away to free up all the reds and yellows of the sand. Amber could feel the sun on her skin, a caress on her cheek, a kiss not yet forgotten. She was moved by the power of life starting all over again, in another morning; the fascination of the sun stepping on the clouds, sending its rays farther and farther; the beauty of the shades running away faster and faster, rolling on each other over the edges of the dunes, hiding from the sun, but not for long. She almost forgot to take pictures, and exchanged some picture-taking favors with a woman that was standing beside her.

- This is so beautiful - Amber couldn't stop herself from whispering.

The woman smiled back at her: - The sunrise is always fascinating from here: this landscape is unique in Namibia, and maybe even across all Africa. When I was younger, the Tsauchab River used to flood the Sossusvlei area once every few years, and we used to come here and canoe in the desert. There used to be much more water here, that's why there are petrified trees in Deadvlei.

The woman warily looked behind their shoulders, down the back of Big Daddy, and gestured towards a smaller salty dry pan, where old petrified acacia trees appeared here and there.

- The sun is always fascinating, but water really brings life here in Africa: rain is our blessing.

- We always complain when it rains in the US: we only see things from our perspective.

Deadvlei left Amber with a strange taste in her mouth: the light hadn't reached it yet, still hidden behind Big Daddy, and the dead white of the ground seemed to annihilate the brightness from the sun. The old acacia trees were dry and lonely, and they couldn't come to life even when the sun finally touched them, a few minutes later. She felt uncomfortable, being there in that cold valley after the reviving warmth of sunrise.

Amber decided to go back to the car.

Breakfast and a long nap at the hotel brought some energy back, and in the afternoon she decided to drive to Sesriem to get something to eat. They didn't have ice-cream there, what she was secretly hoping for, but the local shop had gorgeous books on the animals of the savannah. She bought a pocket guide, promising herself to keep track of the animals that she would encounter, and she held a children's book in her hands for a long time. Mike's brother had a daughter, that Amber had already been calling her niece for a long time, even before they had gotten engaged. The book made her sad: she adored that kid and her sweet smart eyes, but she was probably never going to see her again. She was gone, and there was nothing Amber could do to bring her back, or to bring Mike back. He was gone, too. Everything was gone.

She was tired of having to face that hard feeling in her soul, that sense of complete loss that had originated from Mike's death and that was constantly bouncing back at her. She felt like he was dying over and over again, and she was getting constantly kicked in the face, suffering that overwhelming pain every time something reminded her of him, or a memory of their life together reemerged in her heart. Why did it have to be so hard? Why did she have to keep feeling so miserable?

She didn't buy the children's book.

Amber left the lodge again later that afternoon, to look for a spot to wait for sunset. Colors were bolder, richer; but everything was quieter than at sunrise: that day seemed to have exhausted everyone and everything. A small family of springboks slowly passed by her car, while she was contemplating the sunset sitting on its hood; their white and brown bodies were shining in the fading light. Amber watched them eat some grass and then resume their journey, two younger animals following what she thought might be their parents, all walking together towards the sun.

She felt very lonely.

She waited for the springboks to be far enough, to avoid scaring them when she turned the engine on, and she slowly drove back to the lodge.

8 RISE

Sossusvlei beautifully filled the two days she had left to spend in the area: she went to see the sunrise every morning. She had discovered that she could drive her own car to a parking place not far from Big Daddy, where a sort of public 4WD shuttle would pick tourists up and bring them close enough to the grand dune, exactly where the lodge's driver had left her the first day. Somehow, she never managed to get there early enough not to have to run up Big Daddy, with the pale fear not to make it on time. She always made it, though: it was her daily appointment with Mike. He would be there waiting for her in the soft light of dawn, faithful, eternal. Amber could feel him every morning in the faint touch of the sun on her closed eyelids; she could almost feel him right there with her. It was the best of illusions.

On the morning of the third day, Amber took the road again towards Swakopmund, a small town on the Atlantic Ocean. She drove across deserts and mountains, yellow sand dunes accompanying her for most of the day, her playlist shuffling over and over. She was listening to a playlist that she had created for her wedding day, which contained all her favorite songs: it would have been perfect for the dinner party, she could almost hear people talk and laugh in the background, celebrating her and Mike. There was also a sister playlist for later on, with dance music to make sure the younger guests could have fun after dinner, and keep partying as long as their wedding venue would have allowed them to. She never got to put them up on the given day, but she still liked the selection of songs, and the happy memories they were bringing back with every listening, the deep reasons why she had chosen each one of them. A flashing picture came to her mind: the flowered inner court of the hotel where they were supposed to get married, a magnificent historic building in Old San Juan, Puerto Rico. There was a huge tree in the middle of the court, whose shades covered a swarm of small tables and a beautiful bar; there were terraces at multiple levels that had a magnificent view on the court and there was a small swimming pool at the rooftop level. They had wanted to celebrate their wedding only with their closest friends and families, spending a few days with the quite small group of people they loved the most. They had spent a weekend at the hotel the previous September, to decide on the last details and taste some of the food options: they had been amazed by the place and its ancient but fresh feeling. They had found Old San Juan incredibly authentic and charming. They had loved it all, and Amber had imagined the event and their happiness a million of times since then: she had seen the two of them hand in hand, walking towards a future together, dancing in the moonlight, kissing in the swimming pool the morning after.

Amber realized that her eyes were starting to fog up, and she grabbed her phone to turn the music off, or at least change playlist.

Right at that moment a new song started: the iPhone played a few mandolin notes, and Eddie Vedder's raspy voice started to sing in her ears. "Rise" is a song about life, and the chances you take in it; it's a song about time, and how fast it flows away between your fingers. It is part of the soundtrack of Into The Wild, a movie extremely dear to Amber: it was one of the first films that she had watched with Mike. He had loved the movie so much that they had listened to the whole soundtrack over and over again during one of their road trips, a few years before; the folk allure of the music had been perfect for their summer adventure in the Rocky Mountains. She had loved that song from the first time she had listened to it, and at the same time she had always hated the way it would always make her cry.

It didn't fail that time, either, since Amber was already upset by memories and ghosts of things that would not come. She started to feel that weird sensation in her nose, that sort of tickling inside her nostrils. The feeling slid down in her throat to grasp her chest, and it suddenly became impossible for her to breathe; the frightening sensation then climbed up to the base of her nose and made her forehead wrinkle and her eyes squint. The first tear started to roll down her cheek, slowly. She stopped the car on the side of the road, and allowed herself to shiver and cry.

She hadn't cried in a long time.

> *"Such is the way of the world*
> *You can never know*
> *Just where to put all your faith*
> *And how will it grow?*
> *Gonna rise up*
> *Burning black holes in dark memories*
> *Gonna rise up*
> *Turning mistakes into gold...*
>
> *Such is the passage of time*
> *Too fast to fold*
> *Suddenly swallowed by signs*
> *Lo and behold*
> *Gonna rise up*
> *Find my direction magnetically*
> *Gonna rise up*
> *Throw down my ace in the hole"*

Several hours of gravel road later, Amber reached Walvis Bay, a town a few miles south of Swakopmund, even smaller than its bigger neighbor. Amber's travel guide book had taught her that Walvis Bay was famous all over the world for its unique landscape, and she could confirm it with her own eyes. The desert reached the ocean there, and the dunes seemed to fall directly into the sea, in a sort of eternal battle between water and sand, life and death. It was spectacular.

Mike had chosen a cute bed and breakfast for their stay on the coast. Swakopmund didn't offer much entertainment, if one was not interested in sand surfing or skydiving, but it was a nice road breaker between Sossusvlei and the northern regions of Namibia. Watching the sun setting in the ocean from a pier was a very different experience from what she had had so far in the savannah and in the desert, and Amber felt revived by the sight of the water and the salty smell of the air. She spent a second day in Swakopmund, relaxing on the seaside, visiting the National Museum and looking for souvenirs, and the following morning she took the road to the north again, towards Twyfelfontein.

Amber was more and more surprised by the ever changing landscapes that she was crossing: savannahs and rocky mountains running after each other, dry plains and deserts. She was also more and more surprised, but not in a very positive way, by the roads, which kept getting worse and worse. She was going north, where the majority of the Namibian population lives, close to the Okavango river that represents the key water provision of the country, yet the gravel was becoming bigger and bigger. Stones and rocks appeared in the middle of the road out of nowhere, forcing her to drive slower and slower. She had taken the longest route to go from Swakopmund to Twyfelfontein, to be able to see the Spitzkoppe (one of the highest mountains in the country, almost 6000 feet), but now she was not sure that had been the greatest of ideas. The mountain was worth the detour, though: its red and orange rocks were fascinating in the morning light, and it was absolutely impressing to see the peak emerging from the flat plains that it towered upon.

Amber reached the Twyfelfontein area later that afternoon; the name means "hesitant fountain", and it refers to a local water source known for its non-constant flow. The fountain is anyway strong enough to ensure survival to a various selection of plants and animals, especially one type that Amber had read about in her guide, and that she was more than anxious to meet: the desert elephants.

The lodge that Mike had booked for them was called "Desert Camp", and Amber was curious to see how camping would fit with his idea of a crescendo of beauty and wonder... As soon as she got there, all doubts faded away. She was greeted at the gate by two very young and smiley men, who showed her the way to the lodge. Interestingly enough, she couldn't really see any buildings until she got right at it: the lodge had been built on the side of a red rocky hill, and the cabins had red wood walls and black stone roofs, that perfectly replicated the rocks that surrounded and hid them. Amber parked her car and walked towards the reception building, fascinated by how even the smallest details had been carefully planned by the people who had built the lodge. Lights were hiding behind bushes and rocks, passageways looked very natural, and steps were made of stones. Needless to say, that was no camping.

- Welcome to the Desert Camp, my name is Martha and we're very happy to have you here. Did you have to drive a long way to get here?

- A little bit - Amber smiled back to the young woman who was waiting for her at the reception: that gorgeous place made smiling feel so easy, all of a sudden - I left from Swakopmund this morning.

- Ah the road is not very nice: they have been working on it for a long time.

That was not hard to believe.

- But hopefully you can get some rest here, it's almost sunset time and we will offer you a drink on our sundeck, when you are ready. But let's see your room, first. You are Mrs. Gillingham, I suppose.

Amber nodded, and she waited for the following where-is-your-husband question.

- Very well, Mrs. Gillingham, you have room number 12: it's the farthest from the restaurant and the reception area, but it is very quiet, and as gorgeous as all our other cabins. You can follow me - Martha left the reception counter and grabbed Amber's luggage, walking up a narrow way that Amber hadn't even noticed. She was glad that Martha had skipped *the* question.

They climbed a few steps and walked past several cabins; in the end Martha opened a door for Amber. The space inside was very large, beautifully decorated and very natural looking, with wood and stone and white curtains. There were chocolates on a small desk, for which Amber thanked Martha right away, and she was awarded a large smile as a reply.

- Come find us at the reception from five pm, and we will accompany you to the sundeck, don't forget.

Amber was more than ready for it, and she used that hour to shower the road away from her skin.

The sundeck was a huge flat stone that had somehow been placed right in front of the setting sun; it was populated by small chairs and pillows, which offered to the lodge's clients all the comfort they needed. With the help of a beer, everything looked suddenly perfect to Amber. The sunset added a touch of magic: the hills and plains all around the lodge fired up with reds and browns in the decreasing light. She felt peaceful up there, only touched by the soft breeze and the gentle light of the dying sun; for the first time in several weeks she didn't think about anything, her mind roaming free in the desert, at least for a few minutes.

- It's not that common to see people here by themselves - A man dressed like a safari guide approached Amber with a smile, while she was having dinner at her table for one, facing the darkness outside the lodge.

Amber looked back at him, not knowing what to say: she had already grown tired of the travel journalist story, she didn't want to lie, but she didn't want to tell the truth, yet.

- I'm sorry to bother you during dinner, Ma'am. My name is Patrick, I'm the owner of the lodge, and I wanted to welcome you.

- Thank you, this place is wonderful - She replied with relief, swallowing a delicious piece of zebra meat. She had confirmed with the waiter, just to be sure, that the zebra she was eating had been legally hunted, that it didn't come from a National Park, and it hadn't been killed during some irregular or illegal activities. She was not sure how it could be legal to hunt wild animals in Namibia, and she took a mental note to ask about that at the first opportunity; she had decided to trust the waiter, at least for now.

- It is really a magnificent place - Patrick was saying - Especially when I think about my life before I came here: nothing in common!

- What did you do before?

- Oh I used to work in a bank, and my wife worked for the Government: we were in Windhoek.

- And one day you just decided to come here? I wish I could do the same: I live in New York, probably the least relaxing place in the world, especially when compared to this dream.

- I can imagine that! - Patrick laughed an honest laugh - We couldn't stand the city anymore, so at some point we just decided to leave. But I'm sure I would have left much earlier if I had been born in New York City!

Amber had no doubt about it: - I bet! And how do you like your life here?

- It is amazing, and tiring, but it's that good weariness that you feel when you've worked with your hands, when you've done something with your day: your brain never hurts, your heart is always full of energy. We have the sky above us, and the animals around us... Speaking about animals, did you book your activities for tomorrow?

- Ehm, I'm not sure actually: my... ehm... I might have booked something when I made my reservation for the room, but that was several months ago and I can't remember now.

- Let me check - Patrick said, opening the folder he was carrying under his arm - What's your name?

- Gillingham - Saying it out loud was starting to almost feel fine: she guessed she was getting used to its sound.

- Oh, you booked an all-inclusive, but you didn't specify the activities: that was the right choice! You just got here, right? The morning safari will be perfect for you: we leave at five am sharp, we bring breakfast for you, so you don't have to worry; we look for elephants, and we get back by eleven am, maybe 11:30 depending on how lucky we are with the elephants.

- Are we lucky these days? - She was getting excited - The plan sounds great anyway.

- We have been pretty lucky - Patrick added her name on the list - This morning the elephants were really close to the lodge, on the north side of the river, and the group followed them for hours. We'll see tomorrow: they usually stay in the same area for two, maybe three days, and then they decide to move further, to look for food and feel safer. Remember to bring a jacket: the air is quite fresh in the morning, even if we provide blankets.

The air was already pretty cold that night, when Amber walked back to the cabin. Her room had a little terrace that overlooked the plains on the eastern side of the lodge, and she stopped there for a few minutes before going inside: the stars were dazzling. She tried to remember some of the constellations that Tungue had told her about, only a few days before in the Kalahari Desert, but everything seemed hidden so far back in the past. During those few days she had seen so many things, and most of all she had felt so many emotions, recalled so many memories, assisted to so many touching sunrises and sunsets.

She tried to evaluate her overcrowded emotional status, but she found herself completely unable to look inside her heart in that very moment. So be it, she told herself, and she went to bed.

ANNALISA CONTI

9 LIKE A FLOWER IN THE DESERT

Elephants. Amber had seen them at least a couple of times at the zoo but, just like the giraffes in the Kalahari, these ones were different: their eyes were bright, they looked happy with their lives, always on the move.

It turned out the elephants had walked quite a long way during the night and they were now a bit further away from the lodge. The safari guide on the jeep that was carrying Amber and four other people was communicating via radio with two other cars, and they were able to find the elephants about one hour after they had left the lodge. The cars followed their tracks in the sand: footsteps, broken branches, feces. They got lucky, indeed, because there was an entire family: a female with her baby, one older male and two younger ones. They looked so peaceful: slowly walking around, tearing off branches from acacia trees and bushes to stick them in their mouths with their trunks. The elephants didn't seem to be bothered by the cars, but the driver told his passengers not to make noises, and not to move too much: the animals perceived the car as a unique object, a sort of big strange animal, and they wouldn't attack it unless they felt harmed by it. Amber couldn't take her eyes off of them: they were so elegant and bizarre at the same time, with long legs and wide ears, which started to flow free in the air every time they walked a bit faster.

- If you're familiar with the regular elephants, the ones that live for example closer to the Okavango river - The guide was whispering to his passengers - You can see that these ones are skinnier, their legs longer and slimmer. It's because there's not so much to eat here, for them, so they have to move a lot more, and they don't get fat. All their life is spent walking and eating, and sometimes sleeping: they can walk and eat all night and in the morning, to take some rest only when it's too warm to keep moving, and then get going again when the sun goes down. Life repeats itself for elephants, always the same, yet always different. They travel all the time, after all.

It was fascinating, their resilience was impressive; for sure they never got depressed, or they never spent a week in bed without even showering. Amber smiled at herself, and she took a mental note: learn from the elephants of the desert, never stop moving, and be strong.

- Can you see those branches the female is eating right now? That's an acacia tree: the thorns are so long and barbed, but these elephants can eat them as well. They don't digest them very well though, so the thorns come out of their intestines pretty much untouched: this is why the first law of the Twyfelfontein desert is never to drive on elephant's excrements, if you don't want to cut your tires open with acacia thorns…

They followed the elephants for the whole morning, watching them living their majestic lives made of slow meals and long strolls, in what seemed to be the most peaceful and calm of the existences; when the time came, the guide brought his passengers back to the lodge.

Amber continued the visit of the volcanic desert area on her own, only to discover more examples of life pushed at its limit: resilience and survival seemed to be the key concepts of Twyfelfontein.

She took a guided tour of the Petrified Forest: thousands of years ago, in a post-ice age, an entire forest of pine trees had been flooded, uprooted from Congo and carried all the way south to Namibia. Once in Namibia, the trees had been submerged and compressed by dirt and rocks, but they hadn't lost their strength; the weight of the sediments, and the consequent high pressure applied to the trunks, had let the minerals contained in the rocks permeate the trees, and slowly petrify them. In time, several trunks had started to emerge from the ground, and they were now visible in the forest; some of them measured more than two hundred feet, and they still looked solid and alive.

- These trees are strong like us, the people of Namibia - Her young guide, George, was taking Amber on a private tour of the forest: there was no one else around - It can be sometimes very hard for us to survive here: winters are nice and fresh, but summers can be way too warm at times. But we still love our country: it's the place where we were born, and the place where we want to die. I want to travel, to see the world, but I want to come back here one day. Where are you from?

- I live in New York.

- Ah New York! I see it in movies, all the time. Is it cold there?

- Winters can be cold, much colder than here: the temperature we have here today, this is what we get during our summers.

- Oh man! - George mimed a shiver - Does it snow there?

- It does - Amber smiled at him - It can snow a lot!

- Oh I couldn't live in New York... Maybe during summer, yes I would love summer there, but I would need to find another place for winter.

- I've been telling myself the same thing for years, George, trust me...

- Here we are, this is the other thing I wanted to show you - George pointed out a strange plant to Amber, a sort of short agave with some kind of small trunk, from which two long leaves grew, split in multiple sections towards their extremities - This is a Welwitschia, the national plant of Namibia.

He looked at Amber with a very proud smile on his face.

- This is very beautiful - Amber felt she had to say something.

- You're right, but it is most of all very strong. As I was saying before, life in Namibia is very hard, and here in Twyfelfontein it can get even harder. But this beauty - He

continued, kneeling down to touch one of the leaves - She
has meters and meters of roots, to look for water as deeply
underground as possible. Also, the leaves keep growing
during their whole lives, and they can reach several meters of
length: they never rest. But do you know the most fascinating
thing about Welwitschia? Male and female specimens look
for one another and try to get together: it's like a love dance!
As you can see, they don't grow close to one another, since
water is already scarce for one; they grow pretty far from
each other, in very sparse groups where some of them are
male and some are female. But the pollination needs to
happen somehow, so they send love messages around: they
entrust their pollen to insects, wind, and rain, waiting for
magic to happen. And they also push their leaves to grow in
each other's direction, to maybe be able to touch one
another, one day. Isn't it the most romantic thing in the
world?

It was, George was right: that idea of trying to reach
one another all life long, stretching their leaves as far as
possible, sending their roots deeper and deeper in the ground
to survive one more day, without even knowing if they were
ever going to succeed, it was one of the most moving stories
she had ever heard. For once Amber didn't feel like she was
the loneliest creature on Earth.

She enjoyed the sunset even more, that night, with the
light and warm touch of the declining sun on her face;
realizing that she was surrounded by living beings who had
to fight every day for their life, and fight much harder than
her, brought some sort of relief to her despair. That sunset

had brought her a soft peace that lingered with her until the following morning.

Patrick, the lodge owner, was driving Amber and a German couple in another morning safari in search for elephants. The German guy was all focused on his giant camera, apparently trying to find the perfect combination of settings to be sure to take the best possible pictures of the desert and its animals. His newly wed wife was throwing perplexed looks at him, while contemplating their brand new wedding bands with her eyebrows up high on her forehead, in a mix of surprise and uncertainty. Amber grinned and looked away: Right, she thought, Not everything is perfect in marriage.

- There he is - Patrick suddenly whispered - Try not to move: he's alone, so he's either old and tired or young and aggressive.

It turned out the elephant was an old guy, who chewed his branches even slower than the rest of his family was doing on the previous day. Amber liked to think about them in human ways, and she imagined the old elephant looking like her own grandfather, in one of the few memories of him that she still had: reading a newspaper while sitting on an armchair, with his glasses on the tip of his nose and one hand scratching his head from time to time. The result was quite unique.

- Old males are usually on their own: the group needs a stronger and younger male to protect females and cubs from dangers and predators, so when a male becomes too old he's usually banished by a younger one. This is life here in Africa: you can never rest.

Amber started to grasp the message of strength and hope that Southern Africa was throwing at her.

She had to keep moving, too, and the following day she left the Desert Camp and its beautifully carved buildings to keep running through her adventure, towards the first big National Park of her trip: Etosha.

ANNALISA CONTI

10 THE KING IS NAKED

She woke up with a text from Rachel:

"How are you? Where are you? Are you eating?"

"I'm good. I'll be in Etosha this afternoon. I'm eating: I just killed a zebra with my bare hands and I'm eating it raw, sharing it with a pack of lions."

"Is it tasty?" Rachel never lost a joke.

"I love it, best raw zebra of my life. I'll get a flamingo for dessert."

"Awesome, send pictures."

Amber finished packing and went to the reception to get her last breakfast at the Desert Camp. She took a panoramic picture of the view and she sent it to Rachel.

"I meant a picture of you, not a copy-paste from Wikipedia."

Amber almost laughed while eating a toast, and she asked a waiter to take a picture of her.

"This is better: at least I know the lions didn't eat you. Too bad, I was hoping to inherit your clothes. Next time."

Mike had warned Amber that Etosha was going to be unforgettable, full of animals of all kinds, but she didn't expect the National Park to be *so* full of animals: she was still outside the gates, when two elephants crossed the road just a few feet in front of her car. She was speechless. She had already seen many elephants in Twyfelfontein, of course, but she had been in a safari jeep, a sort of safe environment: her own fake 4WD car didn't feel that safe to her. But she had to get used to it: Etosha is the only National Park in Namibia where one can self-drive, that's to say drive around, on the tarmac or gravel roads, in one's own car. She was going to spend three full days there, and she was planning to give self-drive a try the first day, to experience some real lonely adventure, and go with the lodge's safari guide the following days.

When she reached the gates of the National Park it was already too late to enter, since the park closed right before dusk and it was going to reopen only at dawn. She made a U-turn and she drove a couple of miles back to her lodge, the Etosha Village. Mike was right again: this was somehow even more startling than the Desert Camp in Twyfelfontein, with flowers and big dining tables in the restaurant, superb decorations in the cabin, and the usual inviting poster bed. Amber was ready for tomorrow and all the new encounters that it would bring; the pocket guide to African animals that she had bought in Sesriem was handy in her backpack. She was determined to stay focused on the countless beauties that were waiting for her past the Park's gate: she hoped that Etosha could live up to its promise and distract her from her grim feelings.

She thought she was ready for it, but she wasn't really. Etosha offered such a richness of landscape and fauna that she couldn't possibly store everything in her mind. She had to continuously leaf through her pocket guide to look for animal names; she couldn't stop taking notes on her phone and snapping a lot of pictures with her camera, to make sure she didn't lose anything.

She saw giraffes eating the tops of trees, and coyly looking back at her with their sweet eyes; she spotted hundreds of zebras, drinking at one of the numerous lakes of the National Park. Some of those lakes were natural and some artificially built by men, to ensure a regular presence of water for the animals. She saw thousands of zebras walking in the plains, crossing roads, eating grass, rubbing their heads together. Beautiful impalas with their long horns, running free and jumping high in the grass; groups of gnus looking for a tree to take a nap under its shades.

She saw a beautiful animal that she had never seen before, and she had to look for it on her guide: an oryx. Light brown strong body, with black tail and legs, white mouth and ears, and those horns: long straight horns, majestic and regal.

She saw a rhino: it was walking in the plain, alone but among so many other animals, zebras, gnus and oryxes. She consulted her book and she decided to call it a black rhino: they're very similar to the white rhinos, and neither is white nor black, but the white ones have bigger heads. It was walking, eating, and looking around from time to time. It started to walk towards her car, it kept eating and looking around, but it was going straight towards her, slow but steady. When Amber decided that it was getting too close, she turned on her car and she slowly drove away. It was beautiful, peaceful and strong: an impressive animal.

She saw birds of all kinds: small red and pink, bigger blue with red eyes, a family of Guinea fowls trying to cross the road without losing any component of the team, a lake full of pink flamingos, a big light blue bird that flew away with large wings.

She had her eyes so full of animal wonders, that she didn't even realize how fast the day had gone by: it was already time to go back to the lodge. Her head and her heart were so filled with emotions, pictures, and amazement that she couldn't think clearly about anything else; inside of her she felt she wanted to be excited and satisfied for the day she had just had, but at the same time she couldn't let herself be happy, she just wasn't able to let herself go. She was very confused when she got back to her cabin, and she decided to have dinner and go straight to bed: hopefully the night will bring more clarity to her feelings.

The following morning she confirmed her decision to take the lodge's jeep, and let the safari guide do the work. Also, the waiters had been talking about lions at dinner, and she hadn't seen any, yet. She was quite happy about it though: she was sure that she would have completely freaked out if she had faced a lion on her own - in her car, but still on her own.

She didn't have to wait for long: they found themselves in an open plane where a few zebras and impalas were drinking at a lake; not far from that early morning activity, a large group of lionesses and cubs were still sleeping. It was unexpected for Amber to see such a big group of predators asleep in the middle of a possible banquet, but the guide explained her that the lionesses might have been hunting all night long, and they most likely had already enjoyed a very early morning meal with their cubs. Slowly, the cubs started to wake up and play with each other; they looked like big goofy cats, biting and rolling over each other. That wasn't fun enough, evidently, because they soon started to try and wake up some of the lionesses, for a bit more entertainment. By the time the first lioness opened her first eye, all zebras and impalas were already far away: they had smelled the danger, and they had all been smart enough to escape while they still had time to.

Some time later, her safari guide received a call from another jeep, as it usually happened, and he suddenly turned back the car to go to a specific spot.

He was there, enjoying some sun and warmth after a long night, maybe spent hunting in the dark and later on eating some succulent zebras, or a tender impala. The lion was there in the small valley, close to a little lake. Laying down all curled up, he didn't move: his head turned left and right from time to time, to monitor the surroundings, his tail was spinning in the air, to release the tension. He yawned from time to time, his mouth wide and open, his teeth shining in the morning sun: he was a magnetic vision for

Amber. He started to clean his front paws like a cat, licking them very meticulously, over and over.

- This is unusual - The guide murmured after half an hour; Amber was sitting right next to him, there was nobody else in the car, and only a few other jeeps around them - He hasn't moved at all, maybe he's hurt.

Amber couldn't believe it: hurt? The king of the savannah? Well, kings are often challenged by wannabes, nothing new there.

It turned out the guide was right: at some point the lion stood up and started to move, evidently limping for a wound in his back right leg. He could hardly walk, it was painful to watch.

- That's the law of nature, Miss: you hunt, you run, you eat, you're hunted and you're eventually defeated. It's a cycle: all animals have to move down all the steps of the process, the hunter always becomes the prey, eventually.

Life is hard in Africa, even if you're a lion. You don't always have food in your plate for dinner, you have to keep hunting or risk to be hunted; you have to make sure you stay perfectly healthy, otherwise your own survival is at risk; struggles are real in the savannah, challenges are always a matter of life or death. Loss is always around the corner, and you have to be prepared for whatever shape it takes: an enemy may hurt you, a prey might escape at the very last second and leave your stomach painfully empty, another predator may come and kill your cubs, or your mate. Amber felt compassion for the lion: she knew what it meant to lose everything, to feel dead. Her one loss, yet a terrible one, had been Mike. Mike had been the most important thing in her life, the one thing that made everything else secondary, not important. Had he been even more important than her own health? Most likely. Than her own survival? Maybe even so: her life with Mike had been everything for her, their dreams and plans for the future had fed her and kept her alive for the previous several years, and now everything was gone. Could she start over? Could she create another life for herself? She didn't know.

The lion kept limping away, and he sat down again under the shades of a tree, for a change.

11 WAR

Amber spent her last day in Etosha thinking about the injured lion: What happened to him? Did he survive last night, without being able to hunt or defend himself? Did he find his lionesses or had they dumped him for a younger and stronger male, for good? She would never know, but that image of the limping lion, hurt but fierce, wouldn't leave her head, and would accompany her during her long drive east on the Caprivi Belt.

The Caprivi Belt is a thin strip of land at the very north of Namibia, a slim prisoner between Botswana and Angola that allows Namibia to have access to the Okavango River; because of the river, the vast majority of the two million inhabitants of the country live in the Caprivi area. Amber was fascinated by the fact that a country almost three times larger than Germany, according to what one of the last guides had told her, had such a small population, especially if compared to the eighty millions of Germany itself. The comparison with Germany had been natural for the safari driver: Namibia had been a German colony between the end of the nineteenth century and World War I, and Namibians still carried vivid memories of their European invaders - and the language was still studied in all the best schools of the country. The most used languages were anyway English and Afrikaans, remainders of the South African administration that had followed World War I, until the independence of Namibia in 1990. Amber couldn't get her head around Afrikaans, a mix of African languages, English, German and maybe even some Dutch.

Driving on the Okavango river bank, Amber crossed a number of tiny villages, small groups of huts, before getting to her destination, somewhere halfway between Etosha and Botswana's Chobe National Park. Many people were walking around and in between villages: children were pasturing skinny cows and goats, hurrying them to cross the road and watching out for cars; they very often waved when a car passed by, with big honest smiles that never failed to impress Amber. Women seemed to be going back to their homes, most likely several miles away, with big food baskets or water containers on their heads, one hand to help the balance. Men were walking in small groups, sometimes just smoking in couples, sometimes accompanied by young kids. People lived in very modest cabins, where most of them most likely didn't even have the things that Amber would consider basic, essential: a strong roof and walls that would survive the wet season. What's essential today?, Amber wasn't sure about the answer, at least there. Maybe essential was to be healthy, and still she wasn't sure people were even healthy there: Do they have doctors? Dentists?, she wanted to know more. She had already spent several days in Namibia, but she had only been to very isolated and touristic areas, where she hadn't had any contact with real people: she was now finding the contrast between the beauty of the landscapes and the poverty of the population more striking than she had thought. She promised herself that she would learn something about it.

Seven hours of road went by, somehow, and Amber reached her lodge on the river; once again she was stunned: the main building and the individual cabins were made of dark wood and glass, a very modern and natural look at the same time. The only three rooms that the lodge counted, all with large terraces overlooking the Okavango River, made it a quiet and unique place.

Amber was accompanied to her cabin by a young man, just in time for sunset: the sky was turning red, and the Okavango River was violet in the warm light. She had seen quite a few sunrises and sunsets by then during her trip, but Africa always has the great power of taking you by surprise. She enjoyed the last rays of the dying sun sitting on her terrace on the river, watching the light playing with the soft river fog, the wind dancing with the tall grass and the canes caressing the calm water. She got lost in her thoughts, accompanied only by her inner sad peace, the soft swishing of the Okavango and the rustling of leaves around her cabin.

Once the sun had completely set, Amber reemerged from her open-eyed dreams, and she walked to the restaurant building to enjoy a candlelit dinner on another terrace over the Okavango.

After dinner the two owners of the lodge, a couple from Johannesburg, explained to Amber the activities available on the following day; the most interesting one, for Amber, was the visit of a village close by. She was looking forward to meet some local people, learn some more details about their lives, and visit their local market. The plan sounded perfect, and Amber enjoyed her sleep with a great excitement in her chest: she had suddenly realized that she was craving for something closer to her, more similar, more human. Not that she had already gotten bored by the animals and the ever changing environment, quite the opposite instead: she was feeling more and more bewildered by her journey, that trip to the end of the world for which she had left everything behind, and that she was facing on her own with a sort of reckless courage. She needed something to reconnect with herself, something that she could touch with her hands, feel on her skin, not just an image of a kudu running in the grass. She was looking forward to talking to genuine local people, and learning what did it really mean to be and live in Namibia.

The following day, Amber and a couple of middle aged Europeans met the two owners, Marcus and Antonia, at the entrance of the lodge, ready to visit the village of Andara.

- We are so close to the Angolan border here - Antonia was saying - Sometimes we can still hear mines exploding on the other side of the river. The war is over now, you don't have to worry, but there are still hidden landmines in some areas, and cows and goats might still step on them from time to time.

Amber didn't know much about the civil war in Angola: Mike had told her something about it several months before, on a Sunday afternoon when he was watching a documentary on it, while Amber was finishing an article on Snowpiercer, an indie Korean movie.

- That's the saddest thing about Africa - Mike had said - The history of all countries is almost the same: Europeans come, colonize and enslave for decades; then there's a war to gain independence, from either British, French, German or Portuguese people, depending on the country; then there's a civil war because different tribes or political factions can never agree on anything. And these civil wars are always the worst: child soldiers, twenty or thirty years of bitter conflicts, and the result is never right. Look at Zimbabwe, look at Angola, Sierra Leone, even South Africans weren't able to accept one another, and they are still suffering what remains of the Apartheid. Even Nigeria had to go through it, and they achieved some kind of democracy only a few years ago.

- No wonder your mom never went back: it must be hard for her to accept her origins, considering that now she feels completely British.

- Right. Even if Nigeria is the biggest economy in Africa, or anyway it's going to pass South Africa soon, there is still a lot to do.

Mike had always been looking forward for Central and Southern African countries to become better places: he had always been following their development and their economies with eagerness, with the hope to see improvements, results. With the dream for those People to have the lives they deserved, the food and medical treatments they needed, and governments that wouldn't abuse and kill them but protect them and make them thrive. Mike hadn't been a dreamer, but a man of belief, that's how Amber had called him sometimes. His eyes had always looked far away every time he had spoken about Africa, a mix of hope, anger, and homesickness.

Antonia and Marcus guided their guests into the village. A very friendly young woman showed them the main square, where people spent most of their time together, especially at night after their meals. She explained them that was the place where the village leaders and committees held their meetings, they discussed what improvements and new regulations were needed, and who should replace a deceased committee member or leader. The election mechanism was not very clear to Amber, but it sounded way more straightforward than the primaries and State-by-State system that the US were stubbornly using.

A second woman showed them her house, a small circular cabin made of wood, with a pointed roof built with canes. The interior was divided into smaller rooms by curtains: the bed that the woman was sharing with her husband was in the first room, and it was an old and thin mattress covered with brightly colored sheets. It seemed that all the cooking and dining happened in the main village building, that faced the main square; all women cooked the food for their own families in the main building, ready to share what they had with those who couldn't provide enough for themselves.

Antonia guided them towards the mill, an old abandoned edifice built on a lake, a memory of the old days and the catholic missionaries that had arrived in Andara at the beginning of the twentieth century. The missionaries had built a little church in the village at that time, and they were still helping to manage the local hospital and a small hostel.

In the market, women dressed in bright traditional colors were selling handmade jewelry made of stones, wood and fabric; young men in jeans and t-shirts (apparently the local fashion imposed very different styles to men and women) were showing their wooden sculptures to the small group of tourists: animals, plates, small stools in giraffe or elephant shapes. Amber bought some black onyx bracelets for her mom and for Rachel, and a small decorative elephant for her new living room, hopefully a lucky charm.

Amber didn't know how to feel after the visit: she still felt like a tourist, who had been walked through the most embellished parts of the village, and she didn't think she had had many valuable insights to the reality of life in a little village in Namibia. She realized she wanted to know more: she could have asked more questions during the tour, but somehow she hadn't felt like it, she couldn't explain herself how or why. Who were those people? What were their struggles, what their happiness? What were they thinking, what were their dreams? She wanted to feel part of something, she was missing that human bonding sentiment, that sense of belonging to a place, of having her own role and destiny in the world. Mike had really taken everything away from her, in a way that she wasn't even able to understand, or face.

Amber spent the afternoon alone on the main terrace of the lodge, trying to read a book whose words were continuously getting mixed up, whose pages Amber would turn backward in multiple occasions, realizing that she wasn't paying any attention to the words she was supposed to be reading. In the end she decided to just wait for the sun to set, her eyes lost in the river, and to wait for the boat tour that Marcus was planning for his guests. He had explained that they would need to remain very close to the shore, not to risk entering Angolan waters, but that wasn't going to be a problem: they would still be able to see hippopotamuses and crocodiles, and some of the hundreds of species of birds that populate the river banks.

He was right, and they had some encounters with yawning hippos, whose friendly-looking chubby shapes hide a very aggressive animal, that every year kills more humans than lions do, and that is able to run much faster than any man. They also met some small crocodiles, warming up on the shores after a long day spent hunting in the water. The most impressive sight was always the sun, though: nothing could be more moving and exciting for Amber than a burning sunset, that never failed to surprise her with its strength and warm passion.

12 REALITY

Amber slept well that second night on the river, cradled by the noises of the wind outside her window. She dreamt of Mike, and for the first time it was not about the night he died: she had a memory, more than a dream, of their first vacation together.

The memory started a couple of months into their relationship:

- I have good news and bad news, which ones do you want first? - Mike asked her at dinner, on a Saturday night.

- Are you dumping me?

Mike laughed so hard he spit some wine in his plate: - No! I said *good* news and a *bad* news, this would be horrible news, a tragedy!

- Right - Amber replied, still very serious - Give me the bad ones, first.

- I will be gone for about a month, five weeks, for work.

- That's it? Where are you going?

- South Korea.

- South and not North? Pussy - She commented with a grin.

Mike laughed again: - Yes, South and not North: I'm not sure McKinsey has any clients in North Korea! I mean, you never know, but I don't think so - He concluded with a smile. His smile was bright and honest in Amber's dream, as much as it had been in real life; a smile that had always brought her comfort and confidence.

- Ok, so you're going to South Korea. Is that it?

- Yes, that's it. I told you it was bad and not horrible! - He took her hand in his - But five weeks is going to be a long time, that's why it's bad.

She looked at him in the eyes, and nodded in silence.

- How about the good ones now, are you ready? - He then asked her.

- Shoot!

- I thought that we could celebrate when I come back.

- Come on, you're not even going to North Korea and you want me to greet you like a war hero when you come back?!

- I see why only your nerdy readers love your sense of humor... - He replied; he grinned when she suddenly slapped his hand, but he winked and kept talking - Anyway, I mean we can celebrate the fact that I'm back after five full weeks with a short vacation, maybe a long weekend or even a week somewhere, what do you think?

She stopped joking, for once: - I think it's a great idea.

- That's it? - He was genuinely surprised - No jokes? No making fun of me? Are you sick..?

- I'm not sick, and I agree I won't like not to see you for five weeks, so you should make it up for this time you're stealing from me. Where do you want to go?

- I thought about Colombia: close enough, great weather, not too many tourists, and a beautiful country to visit.

- Are you a drug dealer? Will you put me to sleep and stick some cocaine bags in my…

- No! - He yelled at her with a laugh, before she could finish her sentence - No cocaine bags anywhere, please. Just a vacation.

She finally smiled: - I have never been, I'm sure I'll love it. Do you want me to look for flights or stuff?

- I'll take care of it.

- This is the man that I like: someone who says "I'll do it" meaning "I'll ask my assistant to do it, of course outside of her paid hours, since this is not for work" - She added with a large grin on her face.

In Amber's dream the scene suddenly changed to a beach, one of the places they had visited during that vacation in Colombia. Amber was lying on a beach chair, while Mike was furiously pacing around her; a very heated conversation was going on:

- I don't really see the issue here - Amber was saying, very calm.

- That's it: you never see the issue, you're always so relaxed and easygoing, you never get mad, you never yell. I need to yell sometimes!

- That's useless, and it's bad for your health: do you know that stroke is one of the main causes of death among young management consultants?

- Don't change topic! I can't believe you didn't tell me this before.

- What, that I had a story with a guy a work? Mike, it was two years ago.

- But you still see him, right?

- Right, I see him twice per year, maybe, in the elevator. We don't even actually talk.

- How can I believe that? What do I know about you? - He started to yell - How can I trust you: you were screwing all the nerds in New York while I was working my ass off as an Associate at work! How can I know that you didn't call him while I was in Korea? That you didn't see him? How can I ever trust you with anything, God knows what you have been doing while I was in Korea, or even on any other night I haven't seen you, since we started dating. How many other guys are you seeing? How many men sleep in your bed on a weekly basis? - He spoke without any pause, and by the time he was done screaming at her he was completely out of breath.

She burst out laughing hard, that contagious laughter of hers: - You kill me Mike! This is so funny!

He was completely destabilized by her laughter: - Why are you laughing now?! - He yelled even louder, his face redder and redder, his hands closed in two solid fists.

She stood up from the chair and she took his face in her hands, looking at him straight in the eyes: - Because you're funny - And she kissed him - And because while you were in Korea I spent every freaking waking hour sending you emails and messages, and thinking about what to bring to this vacation. I even went shopping for lingerie with Rachel, and you know that I hate it because she has such a slutty taste, and she always makes me buy stuff that I'll never wear. I *even* had almost every part of my body waxed... and for almost I mean that only my hair and my eyebrows were not affected, as you had the chance to notice not later than this morning.

He didn't move for a few seconds, he didn't say anything, he barely breathed, looking at her straight in the eyes, his own eyes opening wider and wider, more and more startled. Then he threw his head back and started to laugh, very softly at first and then stronger and louder until tears came down from his eyes. He held her in his arms, than he lifted her up and started to run towards the water, where he threw her without saying a word, just laughing.

- You are the one who needs to refresh his thoughts, not me! - Amber yelled and laughed at him while swimming in the ocean.

- You're right - He replied, and reached her running and swimming.

He took her in her arms again and he kissed her, this time: - You're right - He smiled - I'm crazy.

- You're not crazy: you're a man, you're dumb. Not your fault.

He sighed and pushed her head under the water, then he let her go after a second, to hear her swearing at him and starting to laugh again.

He took her in her arms again, and this time he just looked at her: - I love you - He said. He had never said that before.

Amber woke up with his voice in her ears, and that first I love you deep in her heart: they had said that to each other over and over again, every day of the life they had lived together, and it had become like a mantra to them. It had become the confirmation of their commitment to each other, of their will to be there for one another, to be strong when the other one was weak, to be optimistic when the other one was unsure, to burst out laughing when the other one was mad or stressed out. To be there. That was why they had decided to get married: to sign a contract that would put that commitment in written words, to say it out loud to everyone on Earth and in the skies, in the universe, and anywhere else out there. I love you.

13 MIRRORS

Amber missed the sunrise that day: for the first time since she had arrived in Africa she had decided not to put her alarm on, and the sun was already high in the sky when she finally stepped out of her cabin to enjoy her breakfast on the restaurant's river terrace. She could still feel Mike with her, she was smiling: she realized that she had so many loving and funny memories of him that she didn't need anything else to feel peaceful.

She grabbed her phone from her pocket, and texted Rachel:

"Are you awake?"

"Are you ok?" Her friend responded less than two seconds later.

"Are you getting laid?"

"Yeah I wish..."

"Why are you awake? It's the middle of the night in NYC."

"That thing called work, remember?"

"Sort of." Amber hadn't thought at all about work in the previous weeks.

"Yeah. Did you need anything?"

"Will you get laid after work?"

Rachel replied with a weird emoji with a monkey: Amber had no idea of what it meant, and she tried to decipher it while eating a yogurt.

"Mhm."

"Why so interested in me getting laid? Want a piece of it?"

Rachel started to laugh, and the waiter looked at her with a funny face. Sorry, she mouthed, and she kept typing: "No, you're too old for me, you know I like young ass."

"I so understand you babe."

Amber smiled again.

"Anyway, I have to work here. Did you need anything or just wanted to share your good mood?"

"Just missed you."

"Got it: you're not getting laid."

"Nope. Will you get laid?"

"Eventually." Followed by a fingers crossed emoji.

Amber spent the rest of her day in the car, to reach the most isolated and rustic lodge she had been in, yet. A sort of biodynamic solar-powered oasis had been built in the middle of the swamp created by two small rivers fed by the Okavango, the Kwando and the Linyanti, almost at the border with Botswana.

She had left her car in a dusty open space in the middle of nowhere, where a 4WD jeep was going to pick her and her bags up, as Mike had agreed with the lodge via email. The whole scene looked very sketchy: there was only one abandoned car in the parking area, a very old sedan without tires or windows, and for a long time nobody came from the lodge, even if Amber was perfectly on time for her pickup. When the jeep came, Amber was pretty sure she was going to say goodbye forever to her car, but she shrugged her shoulders and got into the 4WD. The driver didn't speak much during the half hour from the parking to the lodge, and Amber enjoyed the wind on her face and in her ears, and the beautiful sights of the rivers and the grasslands all around her.

The lodge had been built and was owned by an Italian couple, and Amber found it so fascinatingly random. The husband explained her that he had actually been born in Namibia, where his family was living at the time, and where his father used to build infrastructures. His whole family had moved back to Italy when he was a teenager, but somehow that had never felt right for him: he had come back to Namibia after graduating from college. An engineer, just like his father, but with a deep passion for clean energies and bio-integration, as he called it, at some point he had decided to move from Windhoek to the Namibian countryside and build something that he could be proud of. The lodge was completely eco-sustainable: solar powered, with a very efficient water recycling system and food supplies coming from villages close by; internet was turned on only a few hours per day, thing that Amber found absolute genius. The wife, Irene, explained the remaining part of the story: she had met Stefano in Italy during her second year of college, and she was not sure how but he had somehow convinced her to move to Namibia for a few months, to experience something completely unique. Months had turned into years, and the idea of the lodge had spread inside both of them like an unstoppable contagion; then the lodge had been inaugurated, and their first son had been born there a bit more than one year before. Irene looked happy: the honest smile Amber had seen on most Namibian faces, with a zest of Italian mockery.

- You're here by yourself - Irene observed while completing her check-in papers - We were expecting two of you.

- I know, I was supposed to come here with a friend, but he couldn't make it.

- Don't worry Amber, you'll have a great time here: we have dinner all together at the same table, you won't feel lonely. And if you feel lonely you come find me, and we have a drink together.

Amber didn't personally know any Italian people: she had only interviewed Monica Bellucci and a few other actors and directors, but she was ready to love them all for the rest of her life if they were all like Irene.

- You're with us for three days - Irene was still talking - There are many activities here: safaris, boat tours, visits to the village, car and boat combos, … You have actually already paid for an all-inclusive, so you can do everything! How about a sundowner small boat tour tonight? You have a little time to get some rest, come here at 4:30 pm for a slice of cake and a coffee, and leave at five. What do you think?

Amber wanted to hug her: she didn't know what it was about her, but with just a few words Irene had been able to make Amber feel welcome, to feel again part of something, of a community, even if only for a few days. She promised herself to accept Irene's offer of a drink at the first available opportunity: Amber was always going to feel lonely, she didn't have any doubts about that, nor any solutions.

The view from her cabin was impressive: the swamp was limitless all around her, and small river branches created a web of slowly moving water, populated by birds and hippos. The pure blue of the rivers and the sky generated a perfect contrast with the deep yellow of the tall grass and canes that were growing free on the river banks and everywhere in the swamp. Amber was ready for another unforgettable sunset.

She got completely taken by surprise, once again, by the untouched beauty of the place and of the sky above and around her. The sun was still high above them, warm and bright, during the first half of the cruise on the small boat. The zodiac could hold five or six people and that night it was also carrying Stefano, their guide for that evening, and a Dutch couple. They saw and heard many animals around them: a big water monitor lizard swam with them for a short while, its little head and nose barely out of the water, a big tail fluttering behind it. A fish eagle stared at them from a tall branch, its white head even brighter against the brown of its body and the dark green of the tree it was resting on. They stopped for a few minutes to observe a snail-eater bird: it was standing in the shallow water, suddenly plunging its beak in the river to capture a snail. The bird could break the snail's shell and swallow the tasty prey in just a few seconds, a great example of smart evolution and adaptation, the keys to survive in Africa; it flew away on wide black wings. They found hippos playing in a basin, and they stayed far enough not to get to their nerves; they heard and saw small frogs singing, elephants calling from far away, birds whistling to the sun.

They waited for sunset in Stefano's perfect spot: he knew his way around. The river was now completely motionless, and its waters reflected the fuller light of the dying sun, creating mirror images of the trees and canes that were growing above them. Amber couldn't stop taking pictures of those perfect double images: a bush standing on top of its reversed double, a tree with its branches up high and down below at the same time. The sun was setting right beside a big tree; some rays of light filtered by the grass seemed to gently caress the water.

She looked in the water right next to the boat, and she saw her face reflected in the river: she looked at that woman in the eyes, and that woman gazed back at her with a questioning look on her face. Who are you, the image in the mirror was asking, Who are you *really*? What are you thinking? Where are you going? Amber had no response to any of her questions.

They got back to the lodge just in time for dinner. As Irene had told Amber earlier that afternoon, a big table was ready in the middle of the terrace that overlooked the swamp. The air was fresh, no mosquitoes to bother the lodge's dinner, since May is the beginning of the winter season in Namibia.

At dinner, Amber was surprised to notice that most of the guests were Namibians: a family on vacation with two young daughters, a few couples, a small group of middle-aged friends; only exceptions, the Dutch couple and a family of three Americans. The American people, a couple with a teenager daughter, were very excited to chat with Amber, since they hadn't seen many people from the US during their trip. They lived in Alaska and they were eager explorers of any kind of nature and natural environment. Hence their decision to spend two months, the kid's summer vacation, travelling in Southern Africa on a caravan, occasionally ditched for a lodge - but clearly nothing less than a gorgeous eco-friendly lodge.

Amber thought about her summer vacations during her teenager years: mostly spent working at her high school library, except for one very lucky year, maybe junior year, when she had found a job in an AMC multiplex in the East Side of Manhattan. She had loved how she had always been able to sneak into a theater to watch a movie, at least a few times per week. She had always loved movies, but that summer had given her the idea that maybe she could try to make a living out of them - and she had ended up majoring in journalism in college, and later on finding a job at Vanity Fair. Somehow that summer had brought her to meet Mike, that night at that party, and she knew she was always going to cherish that memory: many years of happiness had started right at that party. And then the biggest grief of her life. Amber still wanted to believe that the final number at the bottom of her balance sheet was a positive one, might be a very small but still positive one: during her years with Mike she had become who she now was, she had experienced many moments of pure joy. It all had ended with that one call in the middle of the night, but all the cheerful memories were still steadily carved in her heart.

She wasn't going to cherish as much the memory of her short walk in the dark from the restaurant in the main building to her cabin, after dinner: she had had to be accompanied by an armed waiter, a rifle in his hand. That was the main security requirement at the lodge.

- Sometimes lions come hunting in this area at night: they love the tall grass where they can easily hide. You can hear them growling and calling at each other, if you're lucky… Oh, there we are, ma'am, have a good night.

Sure, goodnight to you too.

14 MY COUNTRY, MY PLACE

- Namibia is a beautiful country, beautiful.

Amber hadn't slept very well that night: noises had scared her and kept her awake until very late, so she had decided to sleep in, and go for a safari later in the afternoon. At lunch she shared a table with a Namibian couple and their two adorable daughters: seven or eight years old, the two blonde girls were very politely eating their food, occasionally exchanging a few words in Afrikaans, and listening to their father explaining to Amber a few things about Namibia.

- We have everything here: desert and seaside, savannah and rocky mountains, flourishing National Parks and dead riverbeds. Namibia is a wonderful place for kids to grow up in: we have a farm not far from Windhoek, and trust me when I say that farming in Namibia builds your strength, of body and soul! They love the farm - He kept saying, gesturing at his kids - They are small but strong, and they help me a lot with our cows and goats. They love animals, and they love hunting, as well.

- That's something that I always wanted to ask, since I got here: can you legally hunt in Namibia? - Amber didn't want to lose her chance to ask the question that had been hanging in her head for a few days.

The man smiled: - Of course you can't hunt in National Parks, where all species are protected and hunting becomes poaching. And we all despise it, since it harms species that are already endangered. But there are private game reserves where you can hunt more or less whatever you find, from leopards to elephants, but of course this big game is not very common. You can more likely find zebras and springboks.

- And you can just go and hunt?

- No, I wouldn't say so, regulations are quite strict: you have to go with a qualified hunting guide, of course in a game reserve with all the permits, and you can go only in certain months of the year. You can't hunt everything, either: there are rules that determine the minimum dimensions of the animals you can kill, so that no cubs are injured. And you can also only kill up to two specimens of each animal per year, it's a sort of reverse Noah ark!

- And do you go to one of these hunting reserves with your kids? - Amber was really interested: hunting was completely unknown to her, and she was trying to understand how that could become such a passion for those two apparently harmless young girls.

- Oh no, we have some animals in our own farm, some impalas and some gnus. We all have hunting licenses, we follow the rules. And we kill one or two animals each year, to keep the balance. And, most important of all, we kill them to eat them, not for fun. We honor them, because the food they provide us with can last for several months. We respect them, because they're free and strong, and we kill them with a tear in our eyes. My kids appreciate it because it's our way to thank our Land for the things it gives us, it's the Namibian way: I've been a Namibian for six generations, and this is who we are.

Amber didn't know what to answer: she had never felt such a strong bond with her own Country. Of course she was proud to listen to the National anthem on July 4th, or during the Olympic Games, or right before the Super Bowl, but she wouldn't sing with a hand on her heart like she had seen some old cowboys do at the beginning of rodeos in California or in Texas. There were not many rodeos in Connecticut, though, where she had spent the first few years of her life until middle school, or in New York City: maybe that was the cause of her weaker patriotism.

She didn't know for how many generations she'd been an American, either: three, maybe? She didn't know anything about her great-grandparents: she knew she had some Irish blood (who doesn't, in the US?) and some Swedish or Norwegian. Nobody in her family seemed to know exactly: things were confused before her grandparents. That made her wonder: people always try to get closer to each other during hard times, that was probably why Namibians were so proud of who they were and of the beautiful country they lived in. That was probably also why Amber had felt the deep need of reconstructing some honest human bonds, meeting real people, feeling part of something, once again.

- And our land gives us so much more than animals and food, too - The sixth-generation Namibian was still talking about his Country - But our government doesn't always seem to know what's best for us: all uranium mines are managed by Chinese companies, which ship Chinese workers here, and send all profits back to China. We don't get anything from all these mining activities: no jobs, no benefits for our people and our economy, and the government only keeps a very small percentage of revenues, as a utilization tax. That's all, and it's not a very clever agreement.

Amber didn't want to step into politics, so she tried to go back to safer topics: - And how about other products of your land? It must be complicated to grow anything here.

- It is very complicated! You learn to appreciate every drop of rain the sky sends you. You become the opposite of tourists: you guys all complain when the weather is not perfect here in Namibia, but those are the days we Namibians wait for and welcome with the deepest joy. See, we still live in harmony with our land, we keep the balance: we didn't destroy everything like people have done in Europe, for example.

- In Europe?

- Yes, in Europe: I haven't been to the United States, so I can't say anything about your country, but I have been to Germany a few times; I also brought my family there with me once, to show them what life people have to live there. Do you want to know the most shocking thing? Traffic.

He rolled his eyes in a very theatrical manner, then he somehow found his poise again and he kept telling his story: - Traffic is so unbearable, driving is so dangerous in Germany: too many cars, too many people, everyone is always in a hurry. And the roads are so smooth! No surprise you drive faster and then you get into accidents!

Amber smiled, thinking about her issues with Namibian gravel roads.

- Did you guys have a car accident in Germany?

- No no, we didn't, I was very careful. And of course car crashes happen here, as well, but not because the road is dangerous in itself: sometimes people are in a hurry, they drive too fast and their cars end up upside down. Especially people who work in lodges and take care of supplies: on a given day they have to drive hundreds of kilometers to look for food, or water, and if they are running late and they want to be home before it gets dark, they have to drive faster. And then accidents happen.

Amber had found that lunch not only educational, but also extremely fascinating: Namibia was so much more than a mere safari vacation place, and she now had a better idea of it as a whole. And she could finally understand why Mike had chosen it for the majority of their honeymoon: it wasn't *just* a place with stunning nature, it was nothing like the Kruger Park in South Africa, where tarmac roads bring tourists through almost domesticated cheetahs and yawning lions. Namibia wasn't just a touristic place: it was real, it was fierce, made of actual people; she was sure that Mike had selected some of the lodges to get a chance to have a full Namibian experience, and not just to be pampered and fed.

She loved him even more for that: Mike had always wanted her to see things as they were, to experience and learn with her own eyes. They had travelled the world together, in the years they had known each other, and she had learned to see and watch, to listen and feel. They had gone to India, a couple of years before, and she had seen such poverty there: millions of people fighting for a piece of bread, a handful of rice, living on top of each other. She found that poverty in Namibia had a different look, a sort of dignity given by humanity: survival was increased by proximity, community, mutual help; no one seemed too poor to help someone else. Maybe it was just an illusion, created by the ocean of emotions that had drowned her after Mike's death, maybe it was a facade built for tourists, but she had seen proud and hopeful eyes in Namibian men and women.

She found it ironic: that trip was the perfect summary of Mike's essence, of the things he believed in and that he wanted to know more about. Yet, she was there on her own. But she was doing the best that she could to make it her own trip and get the most out of it, for him as well as for her own self.

After lunch, she sat on an armchair in the lodge's lobby, a covered terrace with sofas and chairs next to the check-in desk. That was the only place in the lodge where the Wi-Fi network actually worked, but Amber had left her phone in her room: she didn't need it. Her parents and Rachel were both fine with receiving a text from her every few days, and not much more. She smiled thinking about the addiction to her iPhone that she had developed through the years: it had been so easy to forget about it, her African rehab was working even too well.

She looked outside in front of her, beyond the terrace's railing, at the sky, the grassy plain, and the trees; she took a deep breath to pull some more Namibian air inside her heart. She opened her guide of Southern Africa, to try to get ready for her next destination, but she didn't even read the first line: Irene appeared with her baby in her arms, and she sat on the sofa right next to Amber.

- He missed you - The Italian girl said, looking at her kid and smiling at Amber - He was wondering where you were: we didn't see you for breakfast.

- I know, I'm sorry I missed your cake - Amber replied, squeezing the little hand that the Italian-born-in-Namibia baby was throwing at her face - I needed to sleep a bit more.

- No worries, you'll see the sunrise tomorrow morning if you go to the combo safari. You have to see it at least once: the sun rises right behind those tall bushes down there, and there's always some pale morning fog that filters the light. It looks like a dream.

Irene smiled, and she asked Amber if she wanted to hold her son, Matteo, for a while. She didn't wait for an answer, and Amber found herself with the baby's big brown eyes stuck into hers. They looked at each other for some long seconds, Matteo's eyes investigating Amber's soul. He then expressed his judgment, in the same way all babies usually did with Amber: he squeaked and started to cry, trying to reach back to his mother.

Irene had a large grin on her face: - I guess you're not that much into babies.

Amber looked back at her, not surprised by Matteo's reaction but still saddened, as if being *almost* married should have somehow improved her maternal instinct: - I guess they're not that much into me, either.

Irene laughed and rubbed Amber's head: - Your time will come, it always does.

Amber was not so sure, not now that Mike was gone and she didn't have anything, anymore, but she decided that she would try to believe her.

She didn't miss her safari that evening: Amber and a Namibian couple took a long ride with elephants and impalas. They also spotted some warthogs, their funny little tails springing in the air behind their backs, while they were running in the sunset.

Most of all, she would have never missed the sunrise combo safari the following morning: a few hours in a jeep and a few more hours in a boat on the river, to capture the full beauty of the marsh at dawn. Elephants were bathing and showering where the river waters were higher; hippos were quietly swimming among the canes, eating and slowly chewing long leaves. Regal impalas with long beautiful horns were running on the grass and in the bushes, from time to time stopping on the river banks to keep an eye on that big strange noisy thing in the water. Amber could swear they were looking at her. Irene was right, as expected: sunrise was pure magic, a revelation of light crawling up from the grass and expanding in the air with warmer and warmer colors. Amber was moved, as sunrise always moved her in Africa: it was always good to remember that life is always stronger than darkness, that everything comes and goes, and always comes back to where everything had started. Nothing was final until it was finished, that seemed to be the message that every sunrise tried to convey to Amber: there should always be some hope left, even just a little fragment of it. She was not sure where to find it, though.

She enjoyed another afternoon in the lodge, another chat with Irene and a dinner with some new faces at the table. While eating, the idea of having to leave the following morning brought her mixed feelings: on one side, she didn't want to abandon that place where she felt so peaceful, far from everything and isolated from everyone. On the other side, she could already taste the excitement of continuing her adventure in a new country: Botswana.

15 OPEN DRAWERS

Mike had always had a heart-felt connection with Botswana, a country that he only knew from documentaries and movies, but which he had a bright and friendly idea of: a place where women were beautiful and men trustworthy. A place with stunning nature and happy welcoming people, a safe and modern country where tourists never had to worry and could instead freely enjoy the many kinds of pure beauty around them.

Many times had he mentioned Botswana to Amber in the previous months, sometimes even openly discussing its issues, like HIV. Mike had explained to Amber how HIV is a very common disease in many African countries and especially in Botswana, where more than a fifth of the adult population is infected. Despite heavy sanitary efforts made by the government in recent years, the infection rate never started to decline. Mike suffered for them, and he kept hoping for things to get better.

Amber thought about Mike all along the way from the lodge in Namibia to the border with Botswana: she didn't just miss him then, she truly wished he could be there, since he had been dreaming about Botswana for such a long time. She was able to finally let her thoughts go, and even grin, when she reached Kasane, the first big city in that new country: the first thing she saw there was a huge saucy poster advertising condoms. And that was only the first of a long series of ads. HIV is something no one talks about in the US anymore - the world is not that small, after all.

Amber had to leave her car at the airport in Kasane: AVIS only allowed, and clearly not without a huge fee, to drop Namibian cars in Botswana, but not in Zimbabwe, where Amber was headed next. That was a good thing, though, because all travel guides strongly advised against self-driving in Zimbabwe, and they all reported some urban legends of foreign tourists arrested and asked to pay absurd fees to enter or exit the country. She was definitely happy with having a driver while there, and she was sure that Mike, who had arranged all transfers, had picked the best and safest options. She was not worried about Botswana at all, but the idea of entering Zimbabwe on her own, with a driver but still on her own, was starting to make her feel uncomfortable.

- Not now - She told herself while parking her fake 4WD close to AVIS' entrance door - That's for three days from now, far in the future. There's Chobe first, then a ride with a random driver from the hotel to the border, then crossing the border itself, then a second ride from the border to Victoria Falls. And then, if you make it, there will be *The Driver* from Victoria Falls to the lodge. Everything will be good.

She looked at herself in the rearview mirror before leaving the car: her perplexed eyes didn't even convince her own self.

The AVIS employee was a great example of the idea that Mike had of people from Botswana: she was beautiful, with big lively eyes and a startling smile. She was extremely nice, as well, and she offered Amber to drive her to her hotel, which was only a couple of miles away. Once they got to the hotel, the AVIS girl wished Amber a great stay in Kasane, and they waved their hands at each other. The girl made a U-turn from the hotel entrance to go back on the main street, and she left Amber's sight.

Amber was ready for the hotel; she had read on the travel guide that the swimming pool was not to be missed there, and she didn't want to disappoint Mike: for sure he had planned that nice swim after another long day in the car. She smiled thinking about him and their very different ways to enjoy a swimming pool: he would wear his goggles and start swimming back and forth, precise and lean. She would walk into the water, look for a place to sit, and find the laziest way to watch him sweat in the water. She was planning to do the same thing that afternoon, once the hotel employee that had escorted her to her room had left.

- Two things ma'am - The young man told her after placing her suitcase on a chair and before leaving the room - The first one is here in this drawer, it's very important.

She came closer to him and she looked in the drawer, where a multicolored selection of condoms had found its perfect spot. She snickered like a teenager, while he remained very serious.

- Always remember, ma'am, if you need this drawer.

At least people seem to take HIV very seriously here, she thought.

- The second thing is very important, too - He soon added - Always remember to keep the door and the windows shut, even when you're in the room. You don't want baboons to enter and pee everywhere. Because that's what they do, ma'am: they pee everywhere and they steal your food. Once I was walking not far from here, under a tree, and a baboon peed on my shoulder. While I was trying to clean my shirt with a tissue, a second baboon stole my sandwich. I told you: they pee and they steal food. You be careful.

And he left the room, leaving her lost in that pee fascination, without even giving her a few more seconds to tip him. She was already bad enough at giving tips, always trying to fold the bills in her hand, and usually making them fall halfway during the tip-giving handshake gesture. Mike was magnificent at that: his big hands seemed to swallow the money inside their palms, to magically release it only at the contact with the other hand. Impressive. He had tried to teach her many times, but she had never been able to fully master that subtle art.

She changed into her bathing suit, and she threw herself in the pool shortly after, lukewarm pleasure. It was not the same thing without Mike, though, without his regular swimming noises and movements, without him trying to drag her in deeper waters, to force her to swim. She got sleepy after a few minutes, a sensation that didn't abandon her all through that night: from the shower to the dinner table, from the sofa on the terrace to her bed, she felt like trapped in some kind of confused foggy dream. She hoped that some actual sleep could fix her.

She was still feeling dizzy the morning after, but probably because she had woken up at 4:30 am to join a morning safari that had already been booked by Mike. He surely hadn't planned for a traditional or relaxing honeymoon...

At that point she thought she couldn't be surprised anymore: she had already seen elephants, giraffes, lions, rhinos, and all kind of gazelles and impalas and zebras, what more was there to see? Well, she didn't know *how many* elephants live in Chobe National Park: thousands. And they seemed to be so used to humans that they did actually approach the jeep, every time the lodge's driver stopped somewhere to look at them or to let them cross the tiny dusty road. Even baby elephants would come close to the car, if they wanted to eat a few leaves from a branch or scratch their backs against a tree.

The National Park includes the vast plain that the Chobe river floods during the wet season, bringing with its waters thousands of animals: from elephants to zebras, from lions to birds. Driving closer to the river, Amber could flash pictures of hippos bathing and yawning in the water in groups of dozens, walking on top of each other in the shallow water. There were crocodiles enjoying the sun, buffaloes resting and eating in the shades, birds small and large screaming at each other.

She saw the sweetest scene of her trip: a family of kudus waking up not far from the road. The female was breastfeeding her beautiful cub; the male, twisted horns standing fiercely on his head, was carefully watching the scene, sometimes looking at his mate straight in the eyes, an unmistakable loving gaze. She seemed to smile back at him, thankful and proud.

Amber also saw the saddest thing of her trip, only a few minutes later. The driver suddenly stopped the car:

- You have to see this - He was telling her and the three other people in the car, gesturing at a small stone on the right side of the road - It's not very easy to see them.

Amber was not sure what she was supposed to look at, when the small stone suddenly moved: it was almost a sphere, and it strangely seemed to be moving up one of the little dunes that formed the sandy road. She looked closer, and she saw a little insect pushing the stone with great effort: he was walking and pushing and walking, trying to climb all the way up the dune. At some point the stone slid on a side and it started to roll down the dune, and the little guy had to run after it, stop it, and start climbing again, to try to keep going in the direction where he wanted to go.

- See, the things we guys do for you women - The guide was saying, with a large smile - This poor dung beetle needs to make the biggest ball of dung that he can, if he wants to hope to have a chance to conquer his lady. He needs to carry it all the way to her nest, to show her that he is strong, that he can build a bigger and safer nest for her and their future children. But this poor guy seems in trouble: the

130

ball is too big for him; will he ever make it to his princess' castle? He is putting so much effort into it, but most likely a stronger male will either get there first, or perhaps steal his big ball of dung and get the girl.

As we say, a shitty job.

Amber couldn't stop laughing: she imagined the same scene enacted by humans, with Rachel despising the guys with not too big or not too smelly of a shit ball, chasing them away swearing and insulting them. It was hilarious. She took a picture of the beetle with her phone, to send it to Rachel later that afternoon: "Let's hope it doesn't hit the fan" she wanted to write as a caption.

"Very funny", Rachel replied that night.

"I knew it: you didn't get it", Amber texted back almost immediately, while sipping a cocktail on the terrace, after dinner.

"I try not to get into shit, if I can avoid it. You're the one who likes it. Fetishist."

"Haha."

"How are you? Glad to make you laugh - mission: accomplished."

"I'm great, this place is great. Now save this because I'll never write it again: you were right."

Rachel sent back something that looked like a yellow amoeba, but that most likely was a fireworks emoji.

"Yes, let's celebrate!"

Rachel sent a heart.

Amber sent two hearts, and the conversation was over: everything that needed to be said had been said. Rachel knew that Amber was getting back to herself, the exact thing the woman had hoped for her friend, the main reason why she had insisted so much for her to go on that trip.

Amber relaxed on the armchair and she took another sip of her piña colada: she was ok, things were going to get better. Somehow.

16 THE TRUTH, PART ONE

The sunset was a red explosion the following night, a fireball falling into the river among dusty clouds, screaming birds and lazy hippos. Hippos were everywhere that night, swimming around the boat on which Amber was touring the Chobe River, and from where she was being hypnotized by the flaming sky.

When they got back to the lodge's dock, she walked slowly towards her room, savoring her last moments in the lodge and in Botswana: the unknown adventure to Zimbabwe was going to start the following morning. A baboon was looking at her from behind a bush, with perplexed eyes that seemed to ask "Why are you walking so slowly?". Surprisingly, he was not peeing, and he didn't look like he wanted to steal anything at the moment.

The sun came back very quickly the following morning, and Amber was ready to go. Her driver was waiting for her at the entrance of the lodge, ready to explain to her that he was only going to drive her to the border, where she had to cross on her own and then wait for another driver on the other side. Everything looked *really* sketchy now.

But reality was, for once, far better than she had expected. The border between Botswana and Zimbabwe, in that region so close to Victoria Falls, was full of tourists from all over the world. The policemen in the border office were collecting visa fees and making small talk with the tourists; she could hear them greeting people in French and in Italian.

- Ah, the United States of America - The officer shouted when he saw her passport: Amber had met only a few American tourists so far, they must have been quite rare in that part of Africa - Where do you live ma'am?

- I live in New York City - She was not even scared anymore.

- New York City, the Big Apple! Zimbabwe is very different, I hope you like it.

- I'm sure I will, officer.

When she exited the border area on the other side, on her own, she felt like an explorer, an adventurer from the nineteenth century, a modern Sir Richard Francis Burton looking for the sources of the Nile. When she climbed on the bus that would take her to Victoria Falls she laughed hard at herself: what a great explorer, on a bus full of old British ladies who got excited and all tittering at every mile.

- Look, an elephant! - One lady said.

- A baboon!

- A bird, up there!

- The Victoria Falls' sign!

- A Barclays! - Amber couldn't help herself and she sighed at the last one.

The trip was short, and it had felt even shorter thanks to the fine British entertainment. Amber soon reached the hotel where another driver was going to pick her up in a couple of hours, to take her to her last safari destination: a lodge in the Hwange National Park, a few hours outside of the city of Victoria Falls.

The hotel was very close to the falls: from the open air terrace she could see their mist and hear their rumble, and it was fascinating. She didn't have much time to visit the falls right then, so for the moment she was happy with that sneak peek. She was going to leave them for her very last day in Africa, before flying back west.

She decided to follow the concierge's suggestion and explore the hotel's surroundings, where she found a small grocery store, for a morning ice-cream, and a few craft shops. She was looking for souvenirs, something more for her parents and for Rachel, but she didn't like those shops: touristy, expensive, fake; she slowly walked back to the hotel, promising herself that next time, a few days later, she was going to be braver and try the actual market.

- Hello, ma'am, my name is Winston, are you Mrs. Gillingham?

Amber was reading on a bench outside the hotel, and she hadn't even seen him coming. She looked at him with the most lost gaze ever.

- My name is Winston, I am your driver to the Hwange National Park, are you Mrs. Gillingham?

- No, I mean, yes, I am. Hi.

He helped her put her bags in the back of a large grey car, and off they went.

The drive was going to take several hours: Winston was bringing her to a gas station in the middle of nowhere, for just another sketchy-looking step in her trip. There a 4WD car from the Hwange National Park lodge was going to pick her up and drive her to the lodge itself. She was starting to trust all those drivers, though: everyone had been really friendly up to that point. Winston seemed a very nice man, too, and Amber was looking for an excuse to start a conversation with him, to learn something about Zimbabwe: Mike would ask him a million things, she was telling herself, I can't just fall asleep in here.

The excuse came to Amber on its own: they had just left the city of Victoria Falls, when Winston suddenly started to slow down until he had to stop at a roadblock. A very young man, wearing a policeman uniform, asked him something in a language that Amber couldn't even identify. Winston answered, and the two kept chatting, apparently friendly, for a few long minutes. Then he pulled up the window and restarted the car. Amber got closer to him, on her car seat: - What just happened?

Winston looked at her in the rearview mirror and smiled: - Don't worry ma'am, this happens all the time here. The police put roadblocks every few miles around all main cities, to ask tourists to pay some money, some sort of transit taxes. You are lucky I'm here, because I know the law and I know that they don't have the right to ask us for any more money: my car has all the papers in order, my plates are fully valid, and all due fees have already been paid.

- Did he ask you for money anyway?

- He sure tried - Winston smiled again at the rear view mirror - But he was just a boy, and I was right, so he couldn't tell me anything.

- And you're saying that this happens all the time, right? - Amber was not very surprised, after all.

- It does, ma'am: if they see a car with only white people inside, they stop it all the time. If they see white people with a black chauffeur, they stop them most of the times: very often tour guides are not from this area and they don't speak the local language, so they don't understand very well what the police are saying, and they end up paying anyway. But between Victoria Falls and the Hwange National Park everybody speaks the same language, my language, so you won't have any issues with me.

- Are you from the area?

- I was born very close to Victoria Falls, and my family is there: my wife, my children, they live in the city.

- It's a big place, isn't it? Full of tourists.

- It is ma'am - Winston replied - And we love tourists, like you: you bring us money, and food for our families. This is very important for us. We are happy to share our beauties with you, because we know that you don't have anything like this at home, and we're happy that you come from all over the world to see our Country. Where are you from?

- The US, I live in New York.

- Ah New York! I have never been there, but it must be a grand city: tall buildings, many people, I bet you never feel alone there!

- You don't, ever. That's why we decided to come here in Africa for this trip: a complete cut with our present.

- I can imagine. What do you do in New York, if I can ask? - He was very polite, she liked it: politeness is too often underrated.

- I am a journalist: I write for a magazine called Vanity Fair, you might know it.

- I sure do, ma'am, this is very interesting. I am a bit of a journalist myself, I write for a small newspaper in Victoria Falls, local news. For sure it is not as exciting as Vanity Fair, but it is very useful for people in Victoria Falls, when they need something or if they want to know the latest news about their neighborhood.

- Local newspapers are the beating heart of a community, I truly respect them. So you're a journalist and a driver, this sounds like a lot of work.

Winston sighed and looked at her from behind his shoulder, just for a second.

- It is a lot of work, indeed, but I have two children, both going to school, and my wife and I want them to go to university and build a future for themselves. And this takes a lot of money: my wife works as a housemaid in one of the hotels in Victoria Falls, and also as a waitress on a couple of tour boats. We do our best.

- I am sure you are great parents - Amber replied, thinking about what he had just said: not even going to school was a normal thing there; nothing had to be taken for granted, after all.

- How are things in Zimbabwe, nowadays? - She didn't even know much about the bad days, a few years before, but she felt she needed to ask. She wanted to understand what *truly* life looked like there, what was normal and what was the exception, what had a great value and what could be taken for granted, if anything.

Winston took a moment to put his thoughts together.

- Things are getting better now. We have food, we have jobs, tourists are finally coming back, and we need them so much, especially here in Victoria Falls: this is the most touristic area in the country, it drives our economy. We didn't have all these things for many years: we didn't have food, we were killing each other. Those were bad times.

I was young back then: no wife, no children, but I had to provide for my family, my parents and my sister, I had to do everything I could. You know, during the war there was no food in the inner parts of the country, like Harare, which is right in the center of Zimbabwe. There was no food there because there was no economy; no one could work, especially there where the government is. Life was really tough there, at that time: people were fighting, and dying, and everyone was struggling. Things were a bit different here in Victoria Falls: we are so close to the border with Zambia and Botswana that food could usually be smuggled in here, one way or another. But it was very dangerous: you could be caught on either side of the border, arrested, even tortured if you were not on the right side of the border, and never see your family again. I have some friends who never came back, their wives left with children to feed, and nothing to eat.

Winston paused for a second, and bowed his head in honor of those who had been less lucky than him.

- Did you smuggle? Did you take the risk? - Amber whispered, not able to stop herself from asking.

- I sure did, ma'am, I had to! When you know that you have only one chance to survive, you just take it, you do everything you have to do, you take all the risks you can, and you just hope that everything goes for the best. I had to survive somehow, ma'am, my family had to survive, especially my parents who were already quite old: they couldn't have made it otherwise.

Amber's eyes were fogged by a thin veil of tears: Winston's story was horrible, yet he was telling it with a smile on his face.

- But things are better now, as I said: we have food, and I can send my kids to school. That's all that matters.

He stopped for a second, and then started to talk again, as if he had suddenly realized that he had missed something: - Of course we still have the same President, so nothing has actually radically changed, but at least we're not struggling as much.

- Right, the same President, it's been a long time now; how is he?

- Ah ma'am, don't let me say things... He's also my cousin, far away in the family but still a cousin, and I know him personally. I think he had the best interest of Zimbabwe in mind when he took power, but you know how we say: power consumes you. He's been listening to very corrupted people for a long time, he's been dealing with difficult situations, and he got grimmer, he had to grow stronger. And now things are what they are. Don't let me say more - He smiled at her - But let me tell you, this is how we are in Zimbabwe: we all hope for the best, in whichever form it might come.

Amber admired that man: proud and respectful even if navigating through a tough life. She thought about all the struggles that he had to go through, all the heartache for the people he had lost, the sorrow for not being able to take care of his family as he probably wished he could. And yet he still had hope for the future, he was still waking up every day with a large grin on his face, maybe simply happy to be alive. Amber's own grief seemed so small now, compared to the full extent of Winston's life. Maybe that was the reason why Mike had decided to add Zimbabwe to their trip: to wake them up from their privileged life, to make them understand what it meant to be *alive*, what it meant to suffer and to recover.

Mike had always been incredibly more concerned than her by the moral and philosophical aspects of life: he had always asked himself more questions about the meaning of things that happened in life, whereas Amber had always been more empirical - "I don't know the answer to this", she used to say, "But I'm sure there's a scientist somewhere that could respond to your question, or who will be soon able to do so, right after his next discovery".

They had gone on a tour of Florida a few years before; they had mutually agreed on visiting the Everglades and the Keys, and then each one of them had chosen a destination to add to the tour. Amber had picked the Universal Studios and Harry Potter Park in Orlando, for which Mike had made fun of her for about two years, while he had chosen Cape Canaveral. At the Kennedy Space Center, they had watched an IMAX documentary on the Hubble telescope, and Mike had been so impressed by the stunning pictures of the cosmos, that he couldn't stop thinking about the universe.

He couldn't grasp the idea of the universe being infinite, he simply didn't get it, his mind couldn't conceive it, and he had to try to interpret it in a philosophical and religious way. Amber had been more rational about it: if there was a formula that somehow confirmed it and explained it, then everything was fine for her, even if she was not going to be able to fully comprehend the formula itself.

In the same way, she had never asked herself too many questions about life and what should be really important about it, whereas Mike sometimes had gotten lost in his thoughts. Maybe that was what that trip was all about, thinking and understanding. Maybe he had wanted her to see what's true about life, what's the substance of it, to be able to enjoy a true happiness, the satisfaction given by the basic things, the truly important ones.

If so, where to put his death? He had been the one thing that had really mattered for her, the one important point in her life. And she had lost him, also losing herself. But there must be something else, right? Not everything could be completely lost for her. She was still healthy, young, and still had a job - supposedly, considering for how long she had been mute with her editor. She was still living in the biggest and wealthiest country in the world, more or less, the country where dreams can come true, where foreigners from all over the world come to study and work, to have a better life. And on top of that, she was on a marvelous journey across Southern Africa; she had absolutely nothing to complain about. Mike's death had been like losing an arm and a leg to Amber, like abandoning a key part of her body, but she had to keep walking and breathing and thinking, she still had to be herself. And she owed it to Mike to still be herself, to learn again how to live her life, and go on as if he were watching her - and somehow he was, she thought, from the picture of him that would always be alive in her heart.

ANNALISA CONTI

17 THE TRUTH, PART TWO

Amber's thoughts had brought her so far away from the car and from Winston that she hadn't even realized that the car had stopped again. More than three hours had already gone by, and they had reached the gas station where someone was supposed to pick her up from the lodge. No one was there yet, but she had faith in the people of Hwange National Park.

The hotel 4WD arrived a few minutes later; a young man greeted her with water and sandwiches, and he left her just a second to thank Winston, before throwing her and her suitcase in the jeep.

A sandy road brought Amber across plains and bush forests, where the jeep drove by trees, rivers and small side roads for another couple of hours, before reaching the lodge right at sunset. Needless to say, the timing was as perfect as it could be. The view was breathtaking: Mike had exceeded any expectations with that lodge, a very small aggregation of wooden cabins built around a quiet little lake. The dying sun was projecting its red rays on the water and across the lone tree that was standing on the other side of the pond; Amber was watching with fascination while a waterbok, springboks' larger relative, was pacing close to the lake, from time to time bending his head to take a sip of fresh water.

Andrea, the woman who greeted Amber and checked her into the hotel, was the owner: she and her husband Francis were Zimbabweans, who a few years before had bought and remodeled the lodge. The result was stunning: simple, lean, soaked in the wildest African nature and its pure beauty.

Amber didn't even have time to get too startled by the simple perfect beauty of her cabin: pre-dinner drinks were served around the bonfire.

- This is a tradition for us - Francis was saying while sipping a beer. He was a tall blond man, his tanned face deeply furrowed with wrinkles, a gift from all the years spent outside under the Zimbabwean sun - The bonfire always inspires stories and creates bonds.

There were quite a few people, mostly middle-aged; Amber was feeling quite alone.

- What story can you tell us today, Francis? - A woman with a central European accent asked.

- You have more stories than me today! These guys - Francis gestured at the woman and her companion, sitting next to her, while looking at the other people around the bonfire - They saw a couple of cheetahs this morning: this is quite rare here! I hope all of you can see them tomorrow morning: you guys all have the early morning safari, and if we're lucky the cheetahs won't move too much tonight. Have you ever seen a cheetah?

Francis was looking straight at Amber.

- No, never - She replied - I've seen lions in Etosha, back in Namibia, but no cheetahs yet. But I've seen a wounded lion, which I believe is quite rare.

- It is - He smiled back at her - We sometimes see wounded elephants here, but seeing injured predators is incredibly less frequent. You were kind of lucky there.

- What do you do when you see an injured animal? - A British woman asked him.

- It depends: there are two types of wounds, and we treat them very differently. If a wound is inflicted by humans, with a weapon or a trap, we usually rescue the animal, we cure her and we set her free when she is ready. We like to think that, if men weren't here, those animals wouldn't suffer, so we try to pay them back. But if the animal was attacked by another animal, a predator, we decide not to do anything: nature has its delicate balance, and we respect it.

- Even if it's a cub?

- Especially if it's a cub: cubs are the hardest to reinsert in their natural environment after they have been treated in our clinics. We rescue the ones that have been hurt by men, but when they are in our treatment centers they have to spend long periods away from their mothers; very often they are not able to survive for too long once we bring them back in the wilderness. We do the best that we can, but unfortunately that's the law of nature, and you have to obey.

- And if it's a mother? Would you leave the cub alone?
- The British lady kept asking.

- We have to, ma'am: what if that mother elephant was destined to die, but we save her and a month later she kills a young buffalo? Whose life is more important? We don't have the right to answer to this question: we humans are only guests here, this is our philosophy.

Amber liked it very much: guests in a unique home, untouched and wild, where animals were free and lived following their own rules. A Garden of Eden, which needed to be cherished and respected.

Cheetahs are elegant animals, the fastest beings to walk the Earth, slender bodies with deep eyes.

Amber was wrapped in a blanket in the open-top jeep, the following morning, trying to fight the early chill and somehow still take pictures of the incredible sight. Two cheetahs were not too far from the car, one of them lazily resting under the shades of a short tree, the other one pacing in large circles, looking around and sniffing the air from time to time. Amber couldn't tell if they were ladies or gentlemen, and her guide neither: too far to tell for sure, but most likely they were two males. A hunting couple, one of the most effective and dangerous weapons of Africa. Amber didn't see them run or hunt, but she could fully enjoy their beauty, lightly spotted and long legged. They alone were worth the 4:30 am rise.

Animals were not rare at all in Hwange, and Amber got her servings of buffaloes, zebras, giraffes, elephants and whatnot since the first day in the park. She could also assist to the most hilarious fact happening right before her eyes: a giraffe drinking from a pond. For some reason, the giraffe had decided that she didn't want to bend her knees while drinking, so she had to spread her front legs wide open and bend her neck to reach the water with her mouth. Getting up again was even more complicated; Amber didn't know if that was a choice or an anatomical necessity for the poor giraffe.

She also saw baboons, a cute family carefully eating each other's fleas. At least they were not peeing around or stealing humans' food. But maybe those habits were peculiar to baboons in Botswana only, who knew.

Amber could still be moved by the pure beauty of the nature she encountered in her safari: she didn't think that would be possible after so many days and so many different landscapes, but in the end every day was different, every safari location had something stunning that would take her by surprise. That was a good feeling, that amazement; it was like remembering over and over again how marvelous and unexpected can life and nature be. It was a good memento for Amber: how many things still existed in the world to be enjoyed.

That night, dinner was served at a common table, a Southern African lodge tradition that Amber liked very much: the perfect occasion to listen to more stories from local people.

- In our lodge, and in most of the lodges here in Hwange, we work a lot with the local communities - Andrea was telling to her guests - We support the village nearby as much as we can: we helped them build their primary and middle schools, and small centers for emergency treatments, since the first real clinic can be several hours away for them.

Our guests are always very generous, too, and they very often leave us some donations to help the village.

- We usually don't think about it - Blake, one of the safari guides, added - But it's really easy for us to help them: the fee for one school year in the village is thirty dollars, ten dollars per trimester. And not all families can afford it. What is nothing for us, can mean a completely different life for them, because going to school is what makes the difference here. Zimbabwe is a very tough country to live in, even today, and children without primary education don't have a future. They cannot find jobs here, not even as park guards or policemen; they cannot even hope to get away and find a better future, or just any future, somewhere else. They're trapped in a vicious cycle of ignorance and poverty.

Amber was shocked. Winston had given her quite a precise idea of life in Victoria Falls, which in the end is a fairly big town in Zimbabwe, flourishing with tourists; life in the villages seemed so different, so much harder. Thirty dollars for one year of school: she had never made any comparison between her own life in New York and the truth that she was capturing in her trip, but she couldn't stop herself from thinking that she wouldn't even pay for a dinner for one person in New York with thirty dollars. You can pay for two movie tickets, with thirty dollars. A movie date in Manhattan had the same value of one year of school in Zimbabwe: Amber couldn't stop repeating those words in her head. Two tickets for one year in school, one year of a child's life: how many more chances for that same child to have a better life? How many better men could be made with those thirty dollars? How much more could be done for the entire Zimbabwe? Amber felt a new grief being born inside of her, a true sorrow for all the lives that had been lost and wasted because of the war, the conflict in Zimbabwe and all the other ones still happening, every day, across Africa. She thought about all the children that could be helped so easily, all the hope that could be given. And that was not a white savior moment, that was not her skin color speaking for her: that was her heart being wrung out in her chest, and hearts are all the same color - they're all red.

Life is so unjust, that was all she could think of: some things don't mean anything for someone, but they can entirely change somebody else's life. Amber had never felt compelled to charity or humanitarianism before: she had been to a charity gala in New York once, and it had looked and felt so phony that she had promised herself she would have never repeated that experience in her life. She had spent the entire night staring at all those people, including herself, who were paying hundreds of dollars to get in, and donating money whose journey from pocket to pocket was never clear enough to her.

- The risk is always the same - Blake was still speaking - To get back to where we were decades ago, before the current President took power and we all had to suffer everything we had to suffer.

Blake was right, and all the people around the table agreed with him; he was a Zimbabwean, and the love he had for his Country was pushing him to talk about the current situation in those very severe terms. He had studied in Oxford, England, when he was younger, but he had had to come back to Zimbabwe after only a couple of years: he couldn't stand those grey foggy English days. He had too much missed his tall grass, the savannah and the sun bright above it, where men and animals could feel completely free. Zimbabwean humans were much like the animals that populated that land: too free to be tamed.

- Healthcare is the other thing we try to help with, after education and schools - Another night, another conversation around the dinner table, eating a delicious zebra roast - Medical treatments are very often completely out of reach for some of these villages, especially for teeth issues. But we cooperate with a European organization of voluntary dentists who come here for a month each summer, not paid nor reimbursed by anyone, and they provide free care for everyone, in a few villages here around.

- What's most amazing is that these people wouldn't have any access to dental care otherwise - Francis added - They would never see a dentist, because the closest dental clinic is in Victoria Falls, and you all know how far it is from here. And they would have to pay the dentist the equivalent of ten years of school for their children: it's easy to see why they don't even consider going. The voluntary dentists are mostly Spaniards, and they genuinely enjoy their time here, even if they have to pay for their flights and everything else by themselves. Maybe this year we can reimburse a few flights.

He looked at Andrea, and they smiled at each other: - Maybe - She replied - And maybe more will come and help us.

Amber had finished her dinner, and she was still moved by the strength of those people, the lodge owners and everyone who was helping them doing something good for the people of the villages. She had never known that level of dedication, of care, of unilateral love. She felt very small.

Andrea stopped by the armchair where Amber was trying to decide what to do the following day.

- Do you know what you want to do tomorrow? - Andrea asked her with a warm smile.

- I was trying to decide, but I'm a bit distracted: I was incredibly touched by the situation at the village. It is so hard for me to imagine how somebody can live in such a different way, what are the struggles that people have to face here. Because life is really hard here, and people are so brave to keep going on every day, to hold on so strongly to their hopes!

Andrea looked at her with an understanding gaze, and she sat down on the armchair next to hers.

- This is a feeling that many people have here, especially when they come on their own.

- I can imagine - Amber replied - And in my case I wasn't even supposed to come alone, and this is why this is touching me even more. I've been here and in Namibia and Botswana for a few weeks now, and I'm living this journey in a way that is completely different from how I had planned it. I expected a vacation, full of adventures and with a lot of fun; I wanted to be excited and amazed by animals and landscapes, and I wanted to enjoy the quiet comforts of the lodges. I had no idea that this experience was going to make me see a different reality, that it was going to give me new eyes through which to look at life itself in a completely different way. All emotions are so powerful here, so real. Even too real.

Amber didn't even realize that she was crying.

- This is Africa, dear - Andrea touched Amber's arm - Everything is more real here than anywhere else. When Francis and I moved here from Victoria Falls we didn't even know what to expect, and what we found changed us forever: the village didn't have a school, or any primary care supplies. They were illegally hunting animals in the park to eat them, and someone still does, if they're hungry. This is the real life, and I always tell myself that if you can handle this you can handle everything.

- I just wish I didn't have to handle this on my own - Amber replied in a whisper.

- You're not alone here, there's so many of us! - Andrea smiled again and squeezed Amber's hand - And I won't ask you what happened, why you had to come here on your own, but let me tell you one thing that I have learned here: everything contributes to make us who we are. There are good times and tough times, and here the tough times outnumber the good times by far, but we all learn how to make the most out of either. And trust me: the smile of the children in the village can cure any wound, bring hope to everyone. Life keeps going on after all.

Amber smiled.

- Why don't you come to the village with me tomorrow morning? - Andrea asked her, out of the blue - I need to bring some new books to the school, we just received them from Harare. You will meet the kids, you will help me with the books, and you can visit the school.

- I don't want to bother you, you have work to do.

- You won't bother me at all. But you won't have time to go to the morning safari tomorrow, is this fine for you? Have you seen enough animals already?

Amber smiled again: - I have even seen two cheetahs here at Hwange, what can I ask for more? I've seen all the Big Fives!

- Very well then, we leave at ten tomorrow morning. You can have breakfast for once.

ANNALISA CONTI

18 PREPARE TO LIVE

Amber was excited, to say the least. The idea of going to the village, of doing something useful, even if it only consisted in bringing some books to the school, was somehow liberating for her. That visit was giving her that sense of purpose she thought she had lost - somewhere between Mike's death and the profound depression that had followed.

She was right to be excited: the children seemed to have just been waiting for her. Of course they didn't know that *she* was coming, and they didn't have any idea about who she was and what she was doing there: all the celebration was for Andrea and the books and affection that she was bringing with her, but it all very soon expanded to include Amber in its embrace.

The two women reached the village in Andrea's car, and they found a first welcome committee waiting for them at the entrance gates: a class of middle school kids was standing in the school's parking lot with a homemade welcome sign. It said "Welcome Andrea! Thank you very much!" in a big cute font. "And welcome Andrea's friend" had been added below, smaller but at least as cute. It made Amber smile, and all the kids threw even bigger smiles right back at her. She understood right away what Andrea had meant the night before: those smiles were the most honest, moving and pure thing she had ever seen. There was no malice, no hidden intention, no fabrication. They were in front of her, opening their hearts and thanking her for being there.

- Come on Amber - She just realized Andrea was talking to her - Go there with them and let me take a picture of you!

The kids hugged her and squeezed her in the picture.

Those middle school boys and girls were old and strong enough to help Andrea and Amber with the books, so each kid took a box and carried it to the school.

- This is what we helped them build - Andrea was saying, a proud smile on her face - It's a primary and middle school: children don't need to leave the village to get the education they need, and when they're done here they're old enough to decide what they want to do with their lives. They can go to high school in Victoria Falls, and maybe one day come back here as teachers; or they can get a job as a park ranger or a safari guide, or help manage the school and the village. Quite a few opportunities open up for them once they have this basic education. Which is probably not much compared to what you may get in Europe or in the United States, but it's everything for them.

- You've done such a great job - Amber replied, while panting under the weight of the two boxes she was carrying - They adore you.

- They are my children.

The real party started when the two women entered the first primary school classroom with their boxes full of books.

The children were all standing at their little desks when Amber and Andrea arrived, and they were timidly glancing at the boxes while the two women were putting them on the teacher's table. When the teacher finally smiled and said "You can get your books now", a unison scream of pure happiness erupted from thirty small throats, and it filled the air and the spirits.

- Yellow hair is my favorite.

Amber hadn't realized that a little girl was gently pulling her sleeve. She had the biggest and brightest eyes Amber had ever seen in her life.

- Yellow hair is my favorite - She repeated, with brighter hope in her eyes.

Amber sat down to look at her in her eyes: she must have been six or seven years old. The girl didn't lose any time and caressed Amber's ponytail.

- You are so beautiful - The girl added.

- Me? No I'm not - Amber replied, smiling back at that lovely face - You are really beautiful! Your hair is so shiny and your eyes are so sweet.

The girl's smile suddenly got even larger: - You are very kind. What's your name?

- I'm Amber. What's your name?

- Nice to meet you Amber, my name is Unathi. Can I have a book?

- Nice to meet you Unathi. Which book would you like?

Amber looked at the teacher, Mayla: half of the class would get "Birds of Zimbabwe", the other half would start from "Animals of the Savannah", and they would switch two months later. Mayla agreed to give Unathi whichever she preferred.

The little girl was suddenly pensive: she didn't expect to have a choice.

- I think I already know the animals of the savannah: my dad taught me many things about them. I think I want the birds.

She didn't sound very convinced, but she looked very excited when she opened the book at the first page and she saw a very colored bird, with blue wings, pink and green head and a yellow belly.

- Is this real? - Unathi couldn't believe in something so beautiful.

- It is - Andrea answered - You can find many of them in the southern regions of our country.

Unathi looked at both Andrea and Amber as if they had revealed a secret, or as if they had done a magic trick.

The sincere admiration and respect in that little girl's eyes touched Amber even deeper than she could realize. Unathi's true happiness, driven and sustained by the tiniest things, by the things that life was offering her every day, made the contrast in Amber's chest even more unsolvable - the contrast with the inescapable depression that she had fallen into after Mike's death, with that sense of demise, of no return, that was hunting her. That sense of lost hope, that infinite spiral of defeat.

Does it ever stop?

Amber wanted to stop it somehow. She looked at Unathi once again: the girl was now sitting on Amber's lap with her legs crossed and her eyes completely drowning in the book, and the woman caressed her little head. That touch, that sense of existence on her hand was so real that it surprised her: she hadn't felt part of reality for a long time, she hadn't felt alive for a long time. The only *real* thing in her life had been Mike: now that he was gone, she had to replace him with something else, something that had to be at least as real as he used to be.

Unathi was as real as reality could be, nestled in her arms.

- You didn't say a word since we left the village.

Andrea was right: Amber had spent the first twenty minutes of their ride back to the lodge in complete silence.

- I'm sorry - She replied with a guilty look on her face - I didn't even realize I didn't say anything.

- Don't be. The village has always a very deep effect on people: sometimes they get over-excited and chatty, other times they look into themselves and start asking questions that require silent meditation to be answered. Am I right? - She concluded with a blink.

Amber was surprised by the depth of Andrea's understanding.

- You are more than right - Amber nodded - If you allow yourself to be touched, there's no turning back: those kids just squeeze your heart in their little hands, and leave you with a dry sponge.

- That sounds painful, I'm sorry if you felt uncomfortable.

- Not at all, it's quite the opposite: it's reinforcing the feelings I already had inside of me since yesterday night, and it's really helping me focus again on what's real, and what needs to be a priority in life. I don't think I had it right anymore.

- And now you do?

- I'd like to think I do. I think I didn't remember what it meant to be a human being anymore. You see, I recently lost someone...

- You don't have to talk about it, I don't want you to bring back painful memories - Andrea stopped Amber right away.

- No, that's fine: it's painful but I now believe that talking about it can make it more bearable.

The two women looked at each other for a very long second.

- I recently lost someone, and that made all my world collapse. He was everything for me, and he still is: I won't be able to replace him with anyone else, not in this life. The empty spot he left in me will always be there. I might find another person at some point, one that will just occupy another spot, but never that same one, never another perfect fit. Now that this is clear to me, I can start living again. And trust me, I want a life that makes sense, not a shadow of what I had before.

Amber paused for a second: that was the key. Not a shadow, but something real.

- My problem was that everything I had left in my life had become a pale shadow without him, that's why nothing made sense anymore, that's why living didn't have a meaning for me, not anymore.

And Rachel had understood this so long before me, Amber thought, That's why she insisted on me moving out of the apartment so quickly, and coming to Africa on this trip.

- But now - Amber kept talking, more to herself than to Andrea - I feel like I have something real again: this trip is real, these people are real, Africa is real.

- And I promise this will always be real - Andrea replied - You can go back to New York, but your life won't be the same, Africa will never leave you. Those children's eyes will always stay with you.

- That's what I hope: to bring a piece of Africa back with me, and keep it with me as long as I can.

- I wouldn't worry about that: once it gets to your heart it never leaves, it keeps burning inside of you. It keeps you alive - Andrea concluded with a light touch on Amber's arm, and one of her biggest smiles.

ANNALISA CONTI

19 WATER

Leaving Hwange was very hard the following morning. Amber had cherished every minute of the previous day, coming back from the village: lunch at the common table, an afternoon safari for a last sunset, a beer around the bonfire. She had never been a snob, but that trip kept surprising her minute after minute: the smallest things now made her the happiest.

After a sad but hopeful hug with Andrea, the day went by fast: the jeep ride in the forest, back to the gas station where Winston was waiting for her, left Amber exhausted, and she slept almost all the way to Victoria Falls.

- Do not apologize, ma'am - Winston told her with a smile, when she tried to excuse herself for having collapsed on the back seat - It is a very good sign for a driver if a passenger falls asleep: it means you are a good and smooth driver. It is also a very good sign when the passenger wants to talk to you: it means you are entertaining. The bad sign is if the passenger is well awake, but doesn't want to talk to you...

Amber smiled back at him: - You are a wise man, Winston.

- That's what my wife always tells me!

One of the last activities that Mike had planned for their trip was a sunset cruise on the Zambezi, that very night.

A driver came looking for Amber at her hotel in the late afternoon, and he brought her down to the small dock where a wooden boat was anchored. The boat was a reproduction of the original vessel that Livingstone had used during his exploration of the Zambezi River, or at least that was what the captain told her and the other ten passengers. For some reasons that Amber could not explain, all the passengers came from the US: two couples and two families, and they all started to chat as soon as they recognized each other as compatriots. Amber wanted to enjoy Africa and its nature for a little while longer, she wanted to feel part of it and its life for one last night, and she decided to keep quiet and pretend she was from somewhere else in the world. The landscape and the sweet smell of the air were all she needed to enjoy, conversation would be superfluous: the river banks covered with vegetation, hippos swimming and chewing grass, some crocodiles hunting for dinner. She felt peace, her eyes lost in the horizon and her mind sweetly recalling moments of her trip: the landscapes she had admired, the animals she had encountered, the eyes of the people she had met, and who had touched her more than anything else. She heard the little Unathi laughing in her soul, and she could grasp once again the reality of her hugs, the matter of the child's small hand intertwined with hers.

Then the sun started to slide down in the sky, and everything turned orange in a stunning sunset. The flaming disc reflected itself in the river, creating a shiny golden pathway, from the water to the sky itself. Trees and bushes turned orange, then red, and in the end black, when the show was over and the boat came back to its pier. That was her last sunset in Africa, and Amber enjoyed it with all her being.

The night felt strange to Amber: she had dinner at a table by herself, because she was in a regular hotel, and not in a lodge. No bonfires, no common tables, no connection with other travelers or local people, Amber felt alone and out of place even if the dining room was full of guests: quite an appropriate sensation for her last night in Africa. After all, maybe it was just about time to go home.

Victoria Falls are even more spectacular if one doesn't know what to expect from them, and Amber had no idea. She had been to Niagara Falls with Mike for their first anniversary, and that had been her first and only big waterfall experience. Nothing can be more different: Niagara falls are created by a change in height of the Niagara river bed, in a point where the river is actually very large and open, and the spectacular falls can be seen from near and far in all their power. On the opposite side of the spectrum, the Zambezi river bed is completely crossed by a very deep and narrow fracture in the ground, and all its water hopelessly tumbles down and creates spectacular falls. The incredible amounts of water that get funneled in such a tight space constantly create thick clouds of mist and vapor, that have to climb their way up the canyon. As a result, infinite rainbows populate the waterfalls, from its top and all the way down to the bridge that connects Zimbabwe to Zambia. Due to the tightness of the canyon, the fall itself can be seen only from a few observation points on its south side. People look small, and everyone feels tiny in front of the falls and their uncontrollable natural power.

The mist and the vapor feed the luxuriant vegetation that inhabits the Zambezi river banks, they provide the place with a unique romantic allure, and they create a permanent rain that completely soaks the tourists that walk through the multiple fall observation points on a daily basis. Amber was proudly among them, even if she felt miserable while walking back to her hotel: wet from head to toes, her hair sticking to her face, but grinning with a silly smile.

Amber took her time to shower, pack her bags, and get ready to go to the airport. Ordinary life: she had been better without it.

She needed all her moral strength to take a taxi at the hotel, wait in line to drop her bag at the check-in counter, wait in line to board her plane to Johannesburg, wait in line to board her other plane to New York. But she was ready to go, ready to come home.

She kept repeating in her head the few words that a tour guide at Victoria Falls had told her when she had finished her tour of the falls: Getting soaked by the waters of the

Zambezi River brings very good luck. She knew that was true: after all, water means life in Africa.

ANNALISA CONTI

20 THE WAY BACK

The customs at JFK: when Amber got there she couldn't think about anything worse. Rude airport workers and police officers; exhausted tourists who don't understand what's going on anymore and just dream about their beds in their hotels; lonely tired people who just want to go home. Like her.

- Hello - She said to the border officer.

- Hello - He replied, grabbing her passport from her hands, checking her picture page and finally her face, to confirm that she looked like that image of a person ten years younger than her. He didn't speak, he stamped her passport, the customs form, and he whispered a "good day ma'am", before calling the next traveler at his counter. Amber already missed the friendliness and the honest welcome she had experienced in Africa.

Her bag had already been delivered, at least, and she only had to seize it from the baggage claim area. She kept walking slowly towards the exit, towards the door outside of which a few taxis were waiting for their passengers to jump in.

- Amber! - Someone seemed to be screaming her name. She stopped, she walked back a few feet and she looked around.

Someone screamed again from behind her, and this time she recognized the voice:

- Rachel! - Somehow Amber felt she had to scream back.

Rachel ran into her arms and hugged her like she hadn't seen her in a year.

- I feel like I haven't seen you in a year!

- Really? It seems like one day to me: so much happened, it went by so fast!

- You're such a bitch - Rachel suddenly made an angry face - Are you saying you didn't miss me at all?

- Sure I did - Amber replied, smacking a kiss on her friend's cheek.

- Good. Let's go home, we have a lot to talk about. How do you feel?

- I feel good.

Rachel looked at Amber straight in the eyes for a moment, and then she smiled.

- That's what I wanted to hear, that's my girl!

"Home" was a place where Amber had never lived before. Her mother and Rachel had done a fantastic job with the apartment: it was small, but they had chosen beautiful modern furniture that could perfectly fit. A long kitchen with white cabinets, a bright red sofa and the beautiful console in the living room, a pale wooden bed in the bedroom. They had even placed all the pieces of decoration that Amber had loved the most in her old apartment: a few paintings, coffee tables with lamps, a rug in the bedroom, some pictures of her and Mike.

They unpacked Amber's luggage together; she gave Rachel the bracelets that she had bought at the market in Andara, close to the Okavango River, and her friend also picked a necklace from a small collection of souvenirs that Amber had bought in different lodges. Rachel even opened a bottle of wine: somehow she had also managed to fill the fridge with food and drinks.

That was such a strange experience for Amber: an apartment she had never been to, but where so many things already seemed to have found their place. An apartment where she and Rachel now had to fit the clothes and shoes that Amber had brought back from Africa in her suitcase. It was like entering a hotel room where the previous client had forgotten most of her things: Amber knew that she had all her stuff in her suitcase, but when she opened the closet she found more clothes already in there. Who did they belong to? She didn't feel like those old clothes belonged to her anymore.

- I don't want these things.

- What? - Rachel put the wineglass down and looked at her friend.

- I don't want these things, I don't need them - Amber replied, looking at the dresses in her closet - They belong to someone else, to a person that I'm not anymore. To the person who lost everything, and got lost herself. I'm not that person anymore.

- You don't need to keep them, I can throw everything away, and we can buy new things.

- I don't have any money to buy new things: I haven't worked in two months!

- Whatever, take it as a birthday present.

- My birthday is in six months...

- Very early birthday present, then, plus welcome back present.

They threw away three large trash bags of things: mostly clothes, shoes, but also old magazines, bed sheets, towels.

- We'll go shopping tomorrow - Rachel said in the end, getting ready to go home - I know a lot of cool places here around.

- Tomorrow is Friday, don't you have to go to work?

- I made arrangements - Rachel replied with a blink - Just in case.

- Ok, but I'm busy in the morning.

- And what for?!

- I need to go to work, I need to talk to my boss.

- I told you I'll give you the money! Birthday present, remember?

- I remember, thank you - Amber replied with a grin - I just want to make sure I can pay for the rent, at least!

The apartment had a wonderful shower, and the following morning Amber mentally thanked Rachel for choosing a place with a modern bathroom.

For the first time in more than two months she took care of her hair: hair dryer, brush and flat iron to make her long blond bob shine. Her boss, Lauren, was a very elegant woman, and Amber would have never dared entering her office without a perfect hairstyle, a nice dress and high heels.

Amber had already texted Lauren a couple of days before from Victoria Falls, to plan their meeting: her boss had been sincerely excited to hear back from her, and looking forward to seeing her in person after such a long time.

- You look so beautiful!

Lauren hugged Amber in the middle of her office, a long and friendly hug that made Amber feel at home, again: she had almost forgotten that she did actually like her job, and she enjoyed spending time with those people that she called her colleagues.

Lauren looked at her in the eyes: with her dark hair and black eyes, Lauren had a natural warmth in her face and in her smile that Amber had always loved about her.

- I'm so happy to see you here. I have to confess that for a long time I feared you would never come back.

- Me too…

- But you're here, that's all that matters to me. How are you?

- I'm good, you know? I'm good.

- We were all very worried about you, we all thought about you so much in these past weeks. I was worried that you would get kidnapped or something, on your own in Africa, in Zimbabwe even!

Amber smiled at Lauren's scared face.

- I was always very safe, all the time: the countries I visited, especially Namibia and Botswana, are really great and safe places. People have a special kindness there, a genuine happiness and an incredible ability to enjoy life and face everything it brings, good or bad.

- It sounds like a dream place: I don't know how many people here in New York can say they're truly happy, probably just a few.

- I thought the same while I was there.

It was Lauren's turn to smile.

- There's something different in you, Amber: I know you have experienced things that can change a person forever, but there's more.

- You're right, there's more.

- So, what do you want to do? Venice? Toronto? I'm ready to send you wherever you want to go: I'm sure that Jack will be more than happy to let you choose first. Or even earlier than that: some summer festivals? European premieres? Anything.

- I actually had something else in mind...

21 A NEW BEGINNING

Lost and Found,
by Amber Stevens

"The eyes are the first thing you notice when you enter Zimbabwe: those eyes have seen more than you can imagine, they have suffered from war and famine, they have seen hope disappear, then come back to trick them, and in the end leave them again. Those are the eyes of an injured lion: a strong animal, the king of the savannah, who knows he's now going to die. Those are the eyes of a child walking his goats: eyes that can't see much farther away, whose future is just there, with those goats.

But they are also the eyes of a little girl who reads a new book at school, and she enjoys it as a gift, as something precious. They are also the eyes of two young giraffes looking at the same sunset: their heads close to each other, their sweet eyes looking into the future. The future is full of hope here: you just need to grasp it."

Lauren was reading the article out loud to Amber, from her freshly printed copy of Vanity Fair. The magazine's cover was occupied by the picture of Amber and the middle school kids in the village in Hwange National Park; the eyes of a lion were staring at the reader from the article's first page. Lauren seemed to know the article almost by heart, judging from how she didn't even need to read it from the page anymore: she could almost declaim it.

When she finished the last paragraph, Lauren had tears in her eyes.

- This is so good, Amber, so inspired.

- Well, this is my life, this is me.

- I know - A smile washed the tears away from Lauren's eyes - I honestly wasn't sure of how this would come out, when you told me about it last month. But you see, I should have just trusted you.

- Thank you, you know this means a lot to me.

- And there's more: I personally showed it to Graydon, and he loved it.

- You mean Graydon Carter, the editor?

- Yes ma'am.

Amber wasn't sure if she believed her: she had met Carter in a couple of official occasions, Vanity Fair parties, but she had never really talked to him. She wasn't even sure he knew who she was.

- He knows well enough who you are - Lauren was saying, almost reading Amber's mind - He had also loved your column on Game of Thrones, last year: you know he's a fan of the show. But I didn't want to tell you, I wanted you to keep your fresh style, not to get too excited.

Anyway, now I have to tell you about this because you really created something powerful, and he had a great idea: you should make it a series. I don't want you to leave movies, because I know that's always been your passion, but he wants you to do a series of travel reportages. He found your perspective very unique, he admired your approach to traveling in the most complete sense of the word: plunging into the reality of the country you're visiting, trying to watch and listen and learn. He found it very eye opening. And he also found your photos very moving, very real.

You would be free to decide where to go, and when to go, and he mentioned maybe two or three trips per year? And then it could also become your main, and you could write a book, a blog, anything. What do you think?

Amber didn't know what to say, the idea sounded crazy and thrilling at the same time: she had forced herself (better, Rachel had forced her) to leave on that trip to Africa to honor Mike's memory and everything that he had represented and would always represent to her. Would she be able to find the same passion and look inside herself with the same depth in another trip? Would she feel the same real emotions outside of Southern Africa? Could she become a travel writer, an explorer of the world, or was she just a movie journalist, a professional geek in love with cinema?

She didn't have the answers to those questions, so she just decided to go where her instinct was taking her: she decided to follow life. She decided that her life had to go on, driven by that hope she had learned to look after in Africa: the hope of a better future, of finding happiness all over again, in whatever form it was going to reveal itself. She felt that could be her chance to keep growing that new self that had been born somewhere in Africa, between Namibia and Zimbabwe.

Amber smiled.

AFRICA

ACKNOWLEDGMENTS

The broadest thanks go to Emmanuel, who kept sustaining me and rooting for me during the whole development of this book, and he also encouraged me to tell this story that has such a personal connection with our own lives.

I also wish to thank my team of editors and preview readers, who gave me very valuable feedback on *Africa* before it was finalized and published: Alice, Libby and Martin.

Thank you to all the people we met in the places we visited during our own trip to Southern Africa, and who inspired me in the creation of the characters that Amber meets during her trip: Kalahari Red Dunes Lodge, in the Kalahari Desert; Sossus Dune Lodge and Sossusvlei Lodge in the Sossusvlei area; Cornerstone Guest House in Swakopmund; Mowani Mountain Camp in the Twyfelfontein area; Etosha Village and Mushara Bush Camp in the Etosha

National Park area; RiverDance Lodge in the Caprivi Belt; Nkasa Lupala Lodge in the Wuparo Conservancy area, and the wonderful Micheletti family; Chobe Safari Lodge in the Chobe National Park area; Bomani Tented Lodge in the Hwange National Park; Ilala Lodge Hotel in Victoria Falls.

AFRICA

ANNALISA CONTI

ABOUT THE AUTHOR

Annalisa Conti lives and writes in New York City, where she has been spending the last few years of her life. She is a woman who writes about women, real human beings facing drama and challenges, finding happiness and rewards, succeeding and failing. Normal people.

If you like Jane Austen for her honest humor, Gillian Flynn for her descent into human darkness, and Elena Ferrante for her focus on storytelling, you will find Annalisa's tales wildly entertaining.

Annalisa is the author of ALL THE PEOPLE, a women's fiction novel built around a woman's secrets. Reviewers say "you cannot put it down", it is "capturing reader's attention since the very first lines", and it has a "very deep and accurate psychological perspective".

She is also the author of AFRICA, a women's fiction novel which was an Amazon Kindle #1 in its category. Reviewers say it is a "fascinating" "astonishing" story of a life-changing journey to the end of the world, "powerful and dramatic, and well integrated into this incredible "decorum"".

She recently published THE WRONG DAY FOR A KILL, the first short story in THE W SERIES, the world of W, a superhero like no other. What's unique about W? Get a taste of it in the first adventure.

Find more at:
www.annalisaconti.com
@AnnalisaContiUS
www.facebook.com/AnnalisaContiWriter

Made in the USA
Middletown, DE
08 August 2017